Married to the Rake

Samantha Holt

© 2019 Samantha Holt

Edited by Dom's Proofreading
Proofed by Destini Reece and Em Petrova
Cover art by Midnight Muse Designs

Chapter One

Chloe closed her eyes and inhaled deeply, drawing in the musty scent of pages bound with leather. She opened them to find Joanna peering at her. "What is it?"

Joanna chuckled. "This is the happiest I have seen you all week."

"It *is* the happiest I've been all week," Chloe said with a grin. "I am utterly ready for the Season to be over."

Their friend Augusta joined them, a book in hand. "Unless you find a husband this year, you shall still have to come back for the next Season," she pointed out.

Chloe grimaced. "If my mother has anything to do with it, I will come back for the next, then the next then the next, and the next, even when I am competing with girls at least ten years my junior."

Augusta gave a little shudder. "I do not envy you one jot. I am so grateful to be done with the Season." She sighed. "Well, I *hope* I am done with the Season."

Chloe pursed her lips, uncertain what to say.

Unfortunately, Augusta had been engaged for over two years now, and her fiancé was travelling the world with little regard for her—or for setting a date. No one knew when he would return, and it was beginning to look like he never would, but Augusta could not call off the engagement. If she did, no man would touch her again.

Chloe rather liked the idea of men avoiding her, but Augusta was more the romantic sort, and she deserved a man who truly loved her.

The delicate brunette shrugged a shoulder. "I am sure Henry shall return soon. He cannot stay away forever."

Chloe shared a look with Joanna. It was one of annoyance, though not at Augusta. Both of them were angry at Henry for leaving their friend for so long. Chloe had never met the man or, if she had, she hardly remembered him. She and Augusta had only become friends this Season, after half of their acquaintances had married. The three of them were the few remaining wallflowers left.

Though, calling Joanna a wallflower was a bit of a stretch. The elegant, fair-haired woman was only part of their friendship group due to her recently being widowed. Were it not for her status, she would likely be engaged already. As soon as her mourning time was up, Chloe was convinced she would remarry, but Joanna showed little interest in finding another husband. She supposed she could not blame her, especially when her husband died so suddenly and after such a short marriage.

"If I were you, I would jump on a boat and drag the man back to England," Chloe declared as she ran her finger down the gold lettering on the spine of one of the books.

Joanna shook her head. "You would not."

"Well, I would think very seriously about it."

Augusta sighed heavily. "I am certain he will return home soon."

"You just said that," pointed out Chloe.

"Then it must be true." Augusta lifted her chin, but Chloe spotted the resignation in her eyes.

Chloe hated to be blunt—well, she did not hate to be blunt as such—but she hated to upset her friend. However, Augusta needed to face the truth soon. Sitting and waiting around for Henry was not working. She needed to do *something*. Chloe was not certain what but there had to be something that could be done to persuade Henry to come home. Even her family seemed unconcerned about the time passed. Someone had to do something!

She really wished Augusta would be brave enough and just—

"Blast!" Chloe dashed behind a shelf of books and ducked down low.

"Whatever are you doing?" asked Joanna, parting the books so she could talk to Chloe through them.

"Shhhh. I am not here."

A golden brow rose. "You look here."

Chloe waved a hand. "Go away. Pretend I'm not here."

Augusta peered through the gap too, pressing her cheek against Joanna's. "What is going on?"

Joanna rolled her eyes. "Chloe is hiding for some reason."

"Stop talking to me," hissed Chloe. "He will see me."

"Who?" Joanna turned to look around the bookshop.

Chloe ducked all the way down as Mr. Brook Waverley made his way through the bookstore. She sucked in a deep breath and held it. With any luck, he would not come around the bookshelves. What was the man doing here anyway? Mr. Waverley was no reader. The man was a rake and a rogue and he certainly was too busy seducing innocent women to find time for reading.

She crouched deeper and could hear her friends muttering between themselves about her behavior. Because her friends were so new, they did not know of her relationship with Mr. Waverley.

If it could be called a relationship. Loathing a person did not count as one, did it?

Aware of her heart pounding in her ears, she governed her breath as though he might hear them rasping in her chest. Dare she risk a peek? Had he already gone? Damn him for invading the one place where she could find solace. She loathed London and all that it entailed but this bookshop almost made it worthwhile.

Slowly, she rose.

"Miss Larkin?"

Chloe screamed, dropping the few books she was hugging. One landed on her foot and she hissed out a mild curse. She spun in the direction of the voice and scowled. "Look what you made me do."

A dark brow rose. Mr. Waverley ran his gaze up and down her, making her feel as though she were a show horse ready for sale. No, make that a cow. A clumsy, awkward, fat cow. Somehow, Brook Waverley always made her feel like that.

She was no society beauty with her generous curves and red hair that had a tendency to wash out her pale skin, but she was certainly not a clumsy, awkward, fat cow. However, with the way he looked at her at present, she was almost tempted to let out a loud *moo*.

"I only greeted you, Miss Larkin. I am not sure I can be blamed for you dropping your books."

"You startled me."

His generous lips curved to one side. She didn't like how her gaze fell upon them. He would take it as though she was interested in him. Which could not be further from the truth. He was precisely the sort of man she loathed. One like Augusta's Henry who could not be trusted to stick to a commitment. Tales of Mr. Waverley's exploits were rife amongst society and she had never seen anything to contradict those stories.

"Perhaps if you had not been hiding, you would not have been startled." His green eyes sparkled with amusement.

She curled a fist at her side. Why did this man always have to taunt her so? He seemed to take great delight in riling her whenever they met. It should not happen often but, unfortunately, their family's estates were next to one another. The families were far from friends but naturally meetings did occur because of their proximity to one another.

Chloe lifted her chin. "I was not hiding." She glanced down at the spilled books. "I was, uh, looking for a book."

"More books? Surely you have enough books to last you a lifetime."

"Only someone who is ill read would make such a comment."

Instead of annoying him, her insult seemed to amuse him further. Creases appeared around his green eyes. Mr. Waverley was only a year her senior but he had a worldly look to him. That was likely because he had hopped from bed to bed all around the country. If the most recent rumors were correct, he had been bedding a Spanish contessa. All those nights in various women's arms had probably taught him much about the world.

Not that she was envious, of course. She could think of better ways of learning about the world. Through books, perhaps.

"Here, let me help you." Mr. Waverley crouched down to gather the books she'd dropped.

"Oh no." She lowered to her knees. "That's really not necessary." The last thing she wanted was a Waverley to do her a favor. It would never be forgotten.

She reached for a book and her hand covered his. A strange heat burst up her arm and she snatched her hand back, feeling the heat flow into her cheeks. Shooting to her feet, her eyes blurred, her head feeling woozy for a faint moment. Two strong hands grabbed her arms.

Chloe blinked. That same heat radiated from his fingertips pressing gently into her arms.

"Careful, Miss Larkin. I would not want to see you come to harm." His words were warm and teasing. She did not like them one bit.

"That is a lie," she spat.

His lips quirked again. "I am no liar. And despite the history between our families, I have no ill will toward you."

Opening her mouth then closing it again, she searched around for her friends. Joanna caught her eye and gave a subtle nod. Hastening over, Joanna took her arm and created some distance between her and Mr. Waverley. In an instant, the heat began to dissipate from her body.

"Chloe, it is high time we left. We have much to do," Joanna said sweetly.

Augusta nodded vigorously. "Oh yes," she said stiffly. "We must dash."

Chloe did not even bid Mr. Waverley a farewell as she hastened out of the entrance to the shop, accompanied by Augusta and Joanna on either side. Once they were out onto the pavement and at the corner of the road, Joanna pulled Chloe to a halt.

"Now that we have escaped, can you tell us why on earth you are so uncomfortable around that man?" Joanna asked.

Chloe glanced between both of her friends. She did not mind speaking on family matters and she trusted both of these women, but it was a long, ridiculous tale. She hooked her arm into both of theirs and led them over to Regent's Park, just opposite the bookshop. There, they could sit and hopefully avoid Mr. Waverley as he exited the bookshop. She grimaced to herself. She had not even managed to purchase her books and now she would have nothing to read until she returned to the country.

Sinking onto the bench, she waited until Joanna and Augusta were settled and gave a light cough. "That was Mr. Waverley. Of the Waverley's of Pembroke."

"Ah. I have heard of Mr. Waverley. Talk of his attractiveness was not wrong." Joanna gave a sly smile.

Augusta leaned forward. "There is also talk of him being quite the rake."

"It is true," said Chloe. "He is all of that and more."

Joanna eyed her. "Is that why you wish to avoid him?"

Chloe snorted. "I'm not scared of a rake. I know I have nothing that might appeal to a rake."

"That is not—"

Chloe waved a hand at Augusta. She was sweet and kind and thought the best of everyone—even blasted Henry. But Chloe did not need flattery right now. She knew full well Mr. Waverley would never be interested in someone like her. He preferred the exotic types and confident widows like Joanna. In fact, she was surprised Joanna had not been approached by him instead. If he knew Joanna was newly widowed, he would surely offer a shoulder to cry on.

"The Waverleys are our neighbors," Chloe explained. "It is an extremely long story but to put it briefly—the Waverleys hate us and we hate the Waverleys."

"Hate?" Augusta echoed. "That seems an awfully strong word."

Chloe lifted her shoulders. "I believe we have hated them since around the thirteenth century. And every few decades we get into another argument about something else. The Waverleys are utterly unreasonable."

"Hated them since the thirteenth century?" Augusta shook her head. "That seems an awfully long time to hold onto a grudge."

"Ah, but my family will tell you it is no grudge. There is a boundary dispute between the families, and the Waverleys will not concede even though we are right."

"You are certain of that?" asked Joanna.

Chloe nodded. "I have seen the records. Though I do not think it was always the boundary line that was the issue. A great, great, great great-grandfather at some point did something and we have never agreed with them on anything since."

"Well, if he is as much of a rake and as disagreeable as you say, it is best we avoid him altogether," Augusta declared. "He is certainly not the sort of man a young woman wants to be seen around."

Chloe nodded. She would be happy if she never saw him again. Now if only she could forget how he had touched her and how strange it had felt.

Chapter Two

Brook squinted into the gloom of his father's study. Standing by the curtains, through which a thin sliver of light entered, was Sir Robert.

Brook folded his arms. "Whatever are you doing, Father?"

His father turned. "They've been at it again."

Fighting back a groan, Brook strode across the room, skirting the large stacks of books and old records piled high on floors, tables, and shelves. No doubt his father had been looking at their records—yet again—in the hope of finding proof that the thin sliver of land between the Waverleys and the Larkins was theirs.

"By 'they', do you mean the Larkins?"

His father nodded, then turned his attention to peering back out of the window. Brook rolled his eyes and pulled open the curtain.

"You will not see them from here anyway, Father. Why are you wasting your time?"

"One of the servants said the girl's back. Catherine or Coco or something."

"Chloe," corrected Brook.

He waved a dismissive, age-spotted hand. "Well, anyway, she was seen there."

'There' being the boundary. Brook resisted the desire to take his father by his shoulders and shake him vigorously. This feud was ridiculous and when he inherited his father's estate, he thoroughly intended to put an end to it. Though, if his confrontation with Miss Larkin at the bookshop was anything to go by, he would have a difficult time in doing so. He rather hoped Miss Larkin's younger brother would be more amenable when he became of age.

He took in his father's furious expression. His shoulders were growing stooped with age and his once silvered hair was almost white and thinning. The last thing his father needed to be doing at his age was getting angry over some stupid piece of land.

"Miss Larkin is allowed to walk on her own land," Brook reasoned.

His father grunted. "No doubt she was moving the boundary again. That bloody Larkin moved it last month, and I made sure it was moved straight away."

"Or she could just be enjoying the fine weather."

"Not likely. All Larkins are the same." His father wagged a finger at him. "Stay away from her. She will be trouble, just like the rest of them."

Brook thought back to their meeting in London a few weeks ago, near the end of the Season. The only trouble Miss Larkin could cause was dropping a few books on his toes. The bright-eyed, red-haired girl had a tongue on her and clearly disliked him, but the wallflower was better known for avoiding social interaction than getting into trouble.

His fingers still tingled when he recalled the touch of her gloved hand. He could not stop himself from remembering how her arms felt beneath his fingertips. How odd it was that such a small touch could linger in his mind. He had touched many, many women, in far more scandalous places than an upper arm, and yet he could not remember spending so much time dwelling over a touch.

"I'll tell you what, Father, I shall go and see what she is doing."

"Be careful, Brook, those Larkins are a conniving lot."

Brook grinned to himself. Conniving was not the sort of word he would use to describe Miss Larkin. Annoyed, outspoken, and also appealing, yes. But not conniving.

He set out on foot, unwilling to wait for a horse to be saddled. The estate was modest compared to some but stretched for several acres. The River Wey cut through part of it, leading into the neighboring estate of the Larkins. On the left side of the river was where all of twenty feet was argued over.

When he reached the boundary, he saw that the fence had been moved back to the farthest reaches, so that these twenty feet were now theirs again. If history was anything to go by, the fence would be moved once more in a few weeks back onto what the Larkins believed was the true boundary.

A grin broke across his face when he spotted Miss Larkin. Apparently oblivious to him, she strolled along the line of the river, swinging a stick and beheading flowers along the way. Her simple cream gown was stained at the hems and slightly creased. He could not make out her expression underneath the bonnet, but she looked rather like a woman who had just been laid down in the grass and ravished. Oh, how he hoped her cheeks were rosy too.

"Miss Larkin," he called.

She stilled, bringing the stick to a halt. Slowly, she lifted her head. He saw her expression sour. She turned swiftly, heading back in the direction from which she came. Brook moved quickly, vaulting over the fence that dissected their land and hastening to catch up with her.

"Miss Larkin," he called. When she did not stop, he made a grab for her arm. She came to a halt and whirled upon him. Her pale blue eyes sparked with annoyance. Underneath her bonnet, red curls peeked out. He wondered if it really was true what they said about redheads and tempers. The few freckles scattered across an upturned nose added an innocent look to that anger which made him smile.

"Whatever do you mean by grabbing me?"

"Forgive me, I was trying to get your attention. It seems you did not hear me call your name." He offered a charming smile.

"I heard you well enough." Miss Larkin's gaze landed on the fence behind him. "You should not be on our land. If Father catches you here, he shall bring out the shotgun."

"I shall be but a moment. If you care enough about me not to see blood spilt, then I would ask you to take a moment to speak with me."

She glanced around then huffed. "Very well."

"I searched you out to speak about the border."

She lifted her gaze to the sky. "That border. I am desperately tired of hearing about that border."

"As am I." He clasped his hands behind his back. "That is why I think you and I should put an end to this feud."

She released a laugh. "An end? This feud has been going on since medieval times. What on earth makes you think we could manage such a thing?"

"Well, with your brains and my..."

"Good looks?"

"I was going to say charms." He grinned widely. "I'm glad you think I'm good-looking."

Creases appeared between her brows. "I did not say I found you good-looking. But...but I know there are women who do. But not I. Certainly not I."

"Very well. I am chastened. But that does not mean we should not work together. Even if you do find me hideous."

"That is not what I said!"

"Regardless, I think we could do something to fix this."

She eyed him for a moment then shook her head. "There is nothing that I could say to my father to persuade him. I am certain your father is as stubborn. Besides, why would you want to mend the feud? Do you not want your extra land for when it is yours?"

"So, you admit it is Waverley land?" He smirked.

Miss Larkin folded her arms. "I certainly do not. I have seen the records and it is Larkin land."

"Believe it or not, I do not give one fig about the land. However, my father is ageing and this constant arguing is taking its toll. I would like to see him live out the rest of his days in peace."

A red brow rose. "If you want to give him peace, then perhaps you should look to your own behavior."

"What is that meant to mean?"

"If you need to ask, I certainly have no wish to tell you. It is not something of which a lady should be speaking."

"I had no idea I was speaking with a lady. Perhaps I was fooled by her muddied hems and creased gown." He bowed mockingly. "Forgive me, my lady."

"You are incorrigible."

"Why, thank you."

"You have wasted enough of my day, Mr. Waverley. If you do not mind, I shall bid you a good day." She went to twist on her heel, but he moved in front of her. If she could have shot fire from her eyes, he had no doubt she would have done and singed him to a crisp. "Mr. Waverley!" she cried, frustration tinging her voice.

"I am serious. I wish to put a halt to this feud and I think you and I could do it together."

She stared at him for a few moments. "I do not think you have ever had a serious moment in your life. I am not certain what you think you are doing by mocking me and toying with me, but I have no interest in offering you a moment of my time."

"Surely there's some way I can persuade you?"

"Persuade me to spend time with a rake of ill reputation?" She glanced around. "All it would take is for me to be caught alone with you out here, and my reputation would be ruined. It would be a fine way for the Waverleys to get revenge on the Larkins, would it not?"

"You really do think ill of me, do you not?"

"I have no reason not to. You are a Waverley. Besides which, your reputation is well-known."

"And highly exaggerated."

"There is a grain of truth to every rumor," she said.

He could not deny that. Though many of the rumors were exaggerated, he had enjoyed his time in London since he was a youth. He'd found women easy to come by and enjoyed their company far more than spending time in gentlemen's clubs.

"It seems, Miss Larkin, that you are no better than our fathers. You like to hold a man's previous sins against him."

Her brows rose. "Previous sins? I have it on good authority that those sins are very current."

Brook cursed inwardly. No doubt she had seen the talk of his affair with the contessa in the gossip columns. While he had pursued her briefly, nothing had come of it. Before anything could happen, she had returned to Spain. He doubted Miss Larkin would believe him, though. And even if he had not consummated the relationship, his pursuit of her would not paint him any better in Miss Larkin's eyes, he could see that now.

"I shall persuade you, Miss Larkin." He smiled. "I can be very persuasive."

She straightened her shoulders. "I'm sure you are. But I'm not easily persuaded. Whatever game you are playing, I have no interest in partaking in it."

With that, she turned again, hastening away. As tempted as he was to pursue her, he did not think it would help his cause. But he was not dissuaded. In fact, their confrontation had only increased his interest in joining forces with her. An interest that was, in part, just a little selfish. Miss Chloe Larkin was utterly unlike any other woman he had met and he'd be damned if he would not persuade her over to his side. No woman denied him. Not even the stubborn Miss Larkin.

Chapter Three

The gall of the man. Chloe tugged off her gloves in irritation and flung them down upon her dressing table. Blowing her hair from her face, she bent, both fists upon the table, and eyed her reflection. Just as she thought. Her cheeks were red with annoyance.

To think he expected her to trust him. "Damn that man."

She could still recall his smug look as she left. He fully expected her to fall at his feet and do his bidding. Well, he might be used to every woman in Christendom doing such a thing, but she was not one of those women.

Releasing a long, heated breath, she straightened. What was it with Mr. Waverley and catching her off guard? Could he not run into her tonight, when she was dressed in her finery and no longer had mud-stained hands or wild hair? Though, she supposed that would not help. Mr. Waverley always had the ability to make her feel nothing more than a scruffy scarecrow.

Chloe glanced at the clock on the mantelpiece in the bedroom. Papa was hosting a dinner party tonight and Joanna and Augusta were attending with some of their family members. It was the first time either of her friends had visited her home, despite them all living fairly locally. What a fine distraction it would be from the blasted Mr. Waverley. It had been a couple of weeks since she had seen them last, as neither of their families had left London as swiftly as hers, and she was looking forward to it.

There was a light tap at the door, and Emma, her lady's maid, entered. "I am glad you are returned, miss. We should start getting you ready."

Chloe nodded. "Yes, I'd wager it shall take a while to make me ready for the party."

The maid tilted her head. "You do look rather flushed, miss. Is all well?"

"Yes...No...I ran into Mr. Waverley today."

"Ah." Emma assisted Chloe into her undergarments then gestured for her to sit in front of the dressing table. She ran a brush through Chloe's hair, Chloe could feel the knots the breeze outside had caused. She so wished she had thinner, more maintainable hair. It always seemed to tie up in knots every time she left the house.

"I had heard the young Mr. Waverley was returned," Emma said.

"Goodness knows why. I'm sure he is happier in London. More women for him to seduce there," Chloe said bitterly.

"I hear Mr. Waverley is not well. He has probably returned to look after his father."

Chloe bit back her next retort. Perhaps the man really had returned with good intentions—at least toward his father. He might be a rake and a scoundrel but from what she knew of him, he loved his family. That still did not mean she trusted him. Even the worst of men could love their families.

"Did he speak to you?" Emma asked.

Chloe hesitated. She was not sure why, though. Emma knew of the rift between their families, having served the Larkins for the past six years. If one worked for the Larkins, one could not avoid hearing of the rift or even sometimes getting involved.

"I...yes, briefly."

"Was he very rude to you, miss?"

"Yes. Very."

Though, now she thought about it, it was not exactly rudeness. It was more that teasing attitude that had her riled. He thought himself the best of men and that frustrated her so. Could he not see why she refused to trust him? Not only was he a Waverley but he had a reputation that no one could avoid. There was barely a week when he was not written of in the gossip columns.

"Well, I am sure it will not be long before he returns to London. No doubt there is another beautiful contessa for him to pursue." Emma giggled.

Chloe smiled half-heartedly. She was not certain why the idea of him chasing after yet another exotic woman made her stomach pinch. Probably because she felt sorry for the woman. Another in a long line of conquests. It was probably out of solidarity for her sex that she felt such queasiness about the whole matter.

Emma finished styling her hair and added a few sprigs of flowers into the curls. Chloe turned her head this way and that to inspect it in the mirror and nodded with satisfaction. "Considering I have so much hair, you always do a wonderful job, Emma."

"We had better get you dressed, miss. We do not have much time after doing your hair."

Chloe stood and Emma helped her wrangle her curves into an evening gown. Though the gown was only several months old, it had begun to grow tight around her breasts. Curse the damned things. But they never stopped growing. They always made her feel so inelegant and clumpy. Unfortunately, other people did not help. Especially other men. She always felt their gaze landing on them in surprise—as though they had never seen a pair of breasts in their lives before.

"Emma?" her father called through the door before knocking hard, likely with his walking stick.

"You can come in," Chloe called back.

Papa pressed open the door and stepped through the gap, all bedecked in his finery. He ran his gaze over her and sighed. "I had hoped you were not quite ready yet."

"Why? Whatever is the matter?"

"I have it on good authority that the boundary has been moved again."

Inwardly, Chloe sighed. She knew it was but she had said nothing to her father. The last thing she needed was for him to get angry and go storming down there. She wished he would just give up on the matter and let it be. What a waste of time it was squabbling over such a thin slice of land.

"I need you to ride over and check on it. If it is true, I shall have to send men out straight away. I give that Waverley one second and he will try to gain even more land."

"I do not think that is true, Papa. I am sure it can be left for a day. Besides, as you say I am ready." She indicated down herself. "I'm hardly dressed for riding."

"But you are the fastest rider, Chloe. You have plenty of other gowns. I'm sure you can change as soon as you get back." He gestured vaguely with the stick in his hand. "Or else I shall have to send Freddie."

"You cannot send Freddie. He is not a good enough rider." Her ten-year-old brother would probably love the adventure, but she was certainly not letting him get involved in this whole mess.

Though he was already aware of the argument between the families, she was determined that he would grow up not hating the Waverleys like every other male member of the family had done.

"I shall miss my friends' arrival," she said softly, knowing it was pointless to argue.

"I would go, Chloe, but our guests are arriving anytime soon and I must be here to greet them," her papa explained. "And everyone is preparing for this dinner party. They cannot spare a single second away, apparently."

"I know, Papa," she said on a sigh. She did not wish him to go to the border anyway. If any of the Waverleys were there, it might well start a fight.

Maybe Mr. Waverley was right... No, she shook her head to herself. There was no way that scoundrel could be right.

Chloe paused to give her father a kiss on the cheek. "I will go check what is happening."

So, she knew what she would have to report back. Or else she could lie. But her father would find out eventually. So she had better make a show of going to the border. If she had realised she would be sent on such an errand, she would have reported back to her father already on the state of the border. The last thing she had wanted was for him to be annoyed on the evening of the dinner party, especially when her friends were going to be in attendance.

Oh, why could she not have a normal life?

Riding hard, she reached the border in no time. She brought the horse to a halt before reaching the fence, and her stomach sank. He flashed a grin at her, and she narrowed her gaze as she dismounted from the horse.

"What are you doing here?" she demanded.

"Twice in one day. How lucky I am." Mr. Waverley's grin expanded.

"The fence is as yet unmoved. You do not need to be here."

Mr. Waverley grimaced. "My father has set up a patrol. He was waiting for one of you to come down here, but I did not expect it to be you."

"Well, as you can see, it is me." She gestured down herself. "And now that you've seen that the border is not yet moved you may go."

He moved closer to the fence, propping his elbows on it and leaning over. Chloe kept her distance, maintaining several feet between them. She tried to keep her gaze from his exposed forearms, where his shirtsleeves were rolled up. Unlike her, he was dressed for the occasion and while she should have felt superior in her finery, she felt a fool.

"Are you doing something pleasant tonight, Miss Larkin?" he asked, his lips askew.

Chloe folded her arms as though they might provide some sort of shield against him. How was it he read her thoughts almost exactly? She forced her expression to remain neutral and not reveal any of her surprise. "A dinner party. Some of my friends are attending."

"Yet, here you are, dressed rather inappropriately for riding."

She lifted her chin. "Yes, well, no one else would come."

"But you already knew the fence was moved. Why is it you needed to come again?"

Lord, she hated his smug tone. How she wanted to rip that smile off his face with her bare fingers. "My father wanted me to come," she muttered.

"I see this border matter is becoming quite an inconvenience to you." He moved farther forward. "Join forces with me, Miss Larkin, and we can put an end to this. No more traipsing out in your finery to check on this fence. And, best of all, I will plague you no longer."

Grinding her teeth together, she eyed him. He was not wrong, unfortunately. This border scenario was getting beyond preposterous and here she was missing out on greeting her friends so that she could march back and tell her father and he could get riled. He would have men sent out in the morning to move the posts yet again, but within a week she could guarantee they would be back to where they were originally.

The trouble was, she would have to work with Mr. Waverley to fix this.

"Miss Larkin?"

"Very well," she bit out.

"Pardon?"

"I said very well. I shall do what I must to mend this matter. Though, I do not know what you intend to do. How can we remedy centuries of discord between our parents?"

Mr. Waverley put his feet on the fence then vaulted over, landing as easily on the other side. For some reason, the movement left her a little breathless. She took a few more steps backward, but he closed the gap between them with his long strides.

"As I said, Miss Larkin, with your brains we cannot fail to succeed."

"I fear you rather overestimate my intellect."

"Not at all. I know you sneak away from balls to read books. If one can spend so much time reading books, one surely must have vast intellect."

She peered at him. How did he know this about her? Last time they'd been in the same room together had been a long time ago. It seemed odd to her that he had noticed such a thing.

"So how do we do this?" she asked.

"I have been pondering the matter, and I think it would be beneficial to get our fathers in the same room together."

Chloe shook her head rapidly. "It shall be a bloodbath, surely?"

"When was the last time they even looked at each other?"

She pursed her lips. She could not recall. Their hatred for one another had always been lived out from afar.

"My hope is," he continued, "that when they are in the same room as each other, in a setting where they must only be civil, they might find some common ground."

"They have common ground," she murmured. She stomped her foot on the grass. "This common ground. It has caused so many problems, it is ridiculous."

"Well, it will be a start. With you and I there to manage the matters, I am certain something good will come of this."

Why he was so positive, she did not know. She supposed that was one of the benefits of being a wellborn, attractive man. Very few things prevented him from getting what he wanted. As a curvy woman with unruly hair and an inability to charm others, she was more used to things going the wrong way.

"I fear you are being optimistic, but I shall do what I must. How should we bring them together?"

"You know Mr. Benedict, do you not?"

She nodded. "His estate is some four miles from here."

"Mr. Benedict does love to host a ball. I am thinking we can persuade him to hold one and invite both of our fathers. Though, we shall have to ensure that no news of either's attendance reaches their ears."

"It shall not be easy to keep it a secret. Gossip runs rife in Hampshire."

"While you may think me optimistic, I think you underestimate yourself, Miss Larkin. I have every faith that you shall be able to keep our plans a secret." He thrust out a hand, and she stared at it. "Shake it," he ordered. "And so begins our arrangement."

She stared at his hand for a few more seconds. Not once had she ever shaken a man's hand. That was something gentleman did. Not young ladies. Regardless, she inched out her own hand and let it rest in his. He curled his fingers around hers and moved his arm up and down, taking hers with it. When he released her fingers, that strange tingling sensation was back, and she could feel it yet again sweep up to her cheeks. He withdrew his hand and flexed his fingers, his penetrating eyes dashing over her.

"I shall let you get back to your dinner party. But as soon as the ball is arranged, I shall send word."

Chloe nodded numbly, rubbing the fingers that he had held with her other hand. She found she could not move until he vaulted back over the fence and turned away. Why did she just feel as though she had made a deal with the devil? With all these supposed brains, one would think she would be more sensible than to get into an arrangement with Mr. Waverley. Still, if this meant no more late-night trips to the fence, it would be worth it.

Chapter Four

Brook took the tumbler of whiskey from Benedict and sank onto one of the worn leather chairs in the library. Benedict followed suit, taking a long sip and placing the glass down on the side table between them.

"To what do I owe this pleasure?" Benedict asked.

Brook glanced at his friend. Marriage suited the man. Benedict had been as much of a rake as Brook was reputed to be and his marriage had come as a surprise to many, but Elizabeth was a fine woman and if anyone could tame Benedict, it was her.

"It has been many months since I last saw you. How was the honeymoon?

"Pleasant indeed," he said with a grin. "But I doubt you wish to hear about my honeymoon. What is it you are after, Brook?"

"Can I not visit without an ulterior motive?"

Benedict shook his head. "I can count on one hand the amount of times you have visited me here. I do believe my London house was your preferred port of call."

"Alas, you know me too well. I have come to ask a favor of you."

Benedict lifted his glass and took another sip. "Unfortunately for me, I likely owe you a lifetime of favors."

"Hardly." Though Benedict credited Brook with helping him and Elizabeth come together, Brook could not help feel that it was fate the two people should end up together. Both of them had been friends of his for some time, and both were exceptional people. He was glad to have introduced them.

"However," Brook continued, "if you do feel you owe me a favor, I would be remiss not to take you up on it."

"Get to the point, Waverley. What do you wish of me?"

"You know well of this rift between my family and the Larkins," Brook began.

Benedict nodded. "Who in the area does not? It makes life incredibly difficult living in such a social sphere."

"Well, what if I told you that I intended to mend that rift?"

His friend chuckled. "I would say that you are mad. No one has ever been able to repair the rift between your two families. What makes you think you have a chance?"

Brook allowed himself a smile. "Because I have an ally."

"Ally?"

Brook nodded and took a sip of the whiskey, letting it slide down his throat while he recalled Chloe in her evening gown that molded just so to generous curves. It was not the first time he had noticed her curves and it would not be the last. However, it was the first time they had been alone whilst she was wearing such a garment and he had been afforded the full opportunity to peruse her person. He should feel a cad for doing so but, after she had spit fire and brimstone at him, he could not bring himself to feel guilty.

"Miss Larkin," he said simply.

Benedict released a choked sound. "Miss Chloe Larkin?"

"Indeed." Brook allowed himself a smug smile. He'd known he would have a battle on his hands with her, but she had acquiesced rather more easily than he had hoped.

"If her father hears of this, he shall call you out."

Shrugging, Brook drained his whiskey. "I have done nothing wrong."

Benedict gave him a look. "Yes, but with your reputation, it shall be assumed that you have most certainly done wrong."

"Your reputation was no better than mine, remember," Brook pointed out.

"Thankfully, he is a reformed man," Elizabeth declared, sauntering into the room and snatching Benedict's empty whiskey glass. She poured one of her own and drained it.

"How could he not be, with you as his wife?" Brook said with a grin, standing to greet her properly. "You look as beautiful as ever, Elizabeth. I am glad to see Benedict is treating you well."

She waved away his flattery with a hand. "What is this I hear of you mending the rift between the Waverleys and the Larkins?"

"Well, I shall need your help too, Elizabeth. I hope to persuade Benedict to host a ball."

Elizabeth chuckled. "Benedict will need no persuasion."

Benedict stood. "I might if there is to be bloodshed between the two families."

Elizabeth tapped her husband's arm. "As much as the two families loathe one another, I am sure they would not be so rude as to disrupt a social gathering."

Benedict grimaced. "Lizzie, you have been lucky enough not to have been stuck in the center of these disagreements. Believe me when I say both men are entirely capable of disrupting any event."

"Well, I always said I enjoy a touch of the dramatic," Benedict said with a resigned sigh.

"Thank you. I meant what I said, I owe you."

"Nonsense," said Elizabeth. She perched on the arm of her husband's chair. "Did I hear mention of Miss Chloe Larkin?"

Brook pursed his lips. "Listening at keyholes, are we?"

Elizabeth perfected an innocent look. "Can I help it that you two have loud voices and this room echoes just so?"

"I am working with Miss Larkin," Brook admitted.

Elizabeth arched a brow. "Be careful there, Brook. She is an innocent."

"I am aware of that. Though she is not as sweet as she may seem." He thought back to her rather pointed remarks.

"All I am saying is that should you get caught in a compromising position, it shall be assumed that you did so deliberately." Elizabeth smoothed some lint from her husband's shoulder ,and Benedict took her hand, keeping hold of it.

Brook watched the small moment of affection and the slightest pang struck him. It had to be simply because he was in the country and not in the company of any of the delightful women of London. Nothing to do with wanting that sort of familiar affection. He had plenty of years to think about marriage. One day he would do it, he was certain, but he'd yet to meet anyone he could picture such moments with.

"I will be a gentleman, I swear it," Brook vowed.

"It doesn't matter if you are," said Benedict. "Your reputation will be enough to ensure she is ruined."

"I have no intention of ruining her. And my reputation is greatly exaggerated, as you both know. Do I enjoy women's company, yes? But I have not flitted from bed to bed or seduced virgins or stolen women from their husbands."

Benedict held up a hand. "There is no need to defend yourself to us."

"I know, forgive me." Brook grimaced. He never usually cared what was written about him or what others thought of him. Apparently, Miss Larkin's opinion on him mattered more than he had realised.

"Well, I shall leave you two to discuss the ways of the world." She leaned in to give Benedict a kiss on the cheek. "Try not to get into any trouble."

"Never," Benedict promised his wife.

Brook watched Elizabeth leave then turned to his friend. "I swear you took the only decent woman in England."

"Well, she is the most amazing woman in the world, but there are plenty more out there. Even one for you, I'd wager."

"Just one?" Brook quipped.

"One day, you shall fall hard and I shall enjoy watching it, just as you did with Elizabeth and I."

"I only took pleasure in two friends falling in love," he protested.

Benedict shook his head. "That is a lie. You are happy for us, I know, but you cannot tell me you did not enjoy my lovesick behavior."

"It certainly made for some entertainment," Brook admitted.

"So you cannot begrudge me when I do the same."

Brook sighed. "I suppose I cannot. But before anything of the sort happens, I must address this situation with my father.

This disagreement is taking its toll. My hope is to have this argument finally put to rest so he can do the same."

"Well I wish you luck, Waverley, I really do."

"But you do not think it will be that easy."

"Even with Miss Larkin's aid, a centuries old rift will not be easy to repair." Benedict stood and topped up their glasses before sitting once more. "I will do whatever you need, though."

Brook drained the drink quickly, allowing the alcohol to warm his insides and soothe away any doubt. He didn't think it would be easy exactly but with Miss Larkin's help, he could not fail surely.

They whiled a few more hours away, discussing London and fellow acquaintances, and Brook was grateful to forget the border matter for a while. By the time he returned home, however, his father was waiting for him in the entrance hallway. His cheeks were ruddy, making his white hair and sideburns seem more stark.

"Where the devil have you been?"

Brook finished removing his gloves before glancing at the top of the stairs, where his father waited. Taking the steps slowly, he descended them until he was in front of Brook.

"Well?" his father demanded. "I hear tell that the boundary line has been moved again. I need to have it moved back as soon as possible."

Brook resisted the desire to roll his eyes. "You only checked yesterday, Father."

His father huffed, his creased cheeks turning red. "One day, this shall be yours. That land shall be yours, and I would not have it stolen from you by those upstart Larkins. I would hope you care about your inheritance as much as I do."

"I am grateful for everything you've given me, Father. I care very much about our land. But —"

His father spun on his heel, marching toward the library before Brook could finish his sentence. As Brook followed him, his father muttered to himself. Mostly of how ungrateful Brook was, and how horrible the Larkins were. Brook released a long breath. This feud needed to end. This anger and frustration was not doing his father any good.

Brook pursued him into the library. His father sat by the fireplace and snapped open a book, apparently ignoring his son's presence. Brook put himself directly in front of the fireplace where his father could not avoid him.

"Father, I have no wish to anger you..." he began.

His father snapped the book shut. "Then you would be as diligent at safeguarding your inheritance as you are to enjoying yourself."

"When the time comes, which is a long, long way away, I shall be as diligent as ever, I promise."

His father made a dismissive noise and turned his attention back to the book.

"Perhaps if I understood exactly why you continue this dispute with the Larkins..." Brook had heard many tales of the history between the families, but if he could glean some extra information, something that would help repair the rift, it would be worth listening to his father's side of things.

His father's jaw tensed. He eased the book shut once more and lifted his attention to Brook. "I do not continue this dispute. In fact, I would have put an end to it years ago, if it were not for what a bastard that Marcus Larkin is."

Brook scowled. As far as he knew, Marcus Larkin was well-respected. Was it his father's personal feelings toward him coloring his view of him, or was it something else?

"What do you mean, you would have put an end to it?"

Easing himself out of the chair, his father came to stand beside the fireplace, propping an elbow on it. He stared briefly into the empty grate before glancing at Brook. "I had every intention of settling the dispute over the land when I was a young man. In fact, Larkin and I even discussed the matter."

Brook blinked. "You and Mr. Larkin had a conversation about the land?"

"I was an idealist. I thought we came to an arrangement but I was wrong."

"What happened?"

"He revealed his true nature." His father curled the fist that was resting on the fireplace mantel.

"True nature?" Brook echoed.

"He took the woman I was to marry from me," he spat.

Brook stared at his father for a few moments. This was the first he'd heard of there being any woman other than his mother. As far as he knew, his parents were happily married and there had never been anyone else intended for them.

"Who was this woman? How did he take her from you?"

"The bastard bedded her, he did. Did it deliberately so that I would find them. Then, before she could change her mind, he wed her."

"You were in love with Georgiana Larkin?" Though Brook was sure Miss Larkin's mother was a fine woman, he could not imagine his father having any feelings for her.

His father shook his head. "No. Georgiana is his second wife. Julia died within months of their wedding. Consumption." His shoulders rounded, and he dropped his gaze to the floor.

Brook pressed his lips together. No wonder his father was still angry. Marcus Larkin had stolen his father's first love. Maybe, this was a big mistake. Maybe he should not be repairing the rift at all but should be taking up the mantle himself.

Damn it.

Chapter Five

"Is this what you are looking for?"

Chloe leapt away from the pillar on which she had been resting and gave her mother a sheepish smile. Mama handed over the letter, and Chloe shook her head, recognizing the seal upon it. "It is addressed to Papa."

Her mother pressed her lips together, the corners of her mouth curving slightly. "So why exactly have you been watching for the post every day recently?"

Chloe clasped her hands together. She could hardly admit to her and Brook's plan. While her mother was not wholly involved in the dispute between the families, she had always supported her husband in the matter. She would not take kindly to Chloe meddling.

A knowing glint entered her mother's eyes. "I think I know what is happening."

Chloe shook her head vigorously. "I do not think you do."

Her mother waved the letter. "I heard that Mr. Benedict was holding a ball to celebrate his return from his honeymoon. This must be the invitation."

"Oh really? I had not heard such a rumor."

"You are a terrible fibber, Chloe." Her mother pulled a penknife out of the drawer of the side table and pressed open the seal.

"That is addressed to Papa," Chloe pointed out.

"Oh, he will not mind. He could not give a fig about a ball."

"But he will want to go, will he not?" Chloe cursed herself for her eagerness. Her mother was bound to think something was wrong.

"Do not fear, my darling. I shall ensure he goes." Her mother peeled open the letter and scanned the contents. "I suspect there should be many eligible men in attendance. Mr. Benedict has several friends of good standing." That glint had entered her mother's eyes again.

"Oh no, Mama..."

"Do not worry. I shall not say anything to your father. But, I must admit, I am glad you are finally showing interest in finding a husband. I have been waiting for this day for a long time."

Chloe grimaced. She supposed she understood why her mother would jump to such a conclusion. Why else would she finally be eager to go to a ball? She had certainly never been so before.

"I shall have to ensure that none of the Waverleys will be attending," her mother commented. "Though, they certainly would not be if we are. There is no chance Mr. Benedict would invite both families. He is no fool."

Chloe closed her eyes briefly. Now she regretted getting Mr. Benedict involved in the matter. Both families would be angry at him indeed at being invited. Still, if their fathers made friends, it would not matter at all. Goodness, they might even thank Mr. Benedict.

"I do hope Papa would not make a scene if one of them were there," Chloe said softly.

Her mother gave her a look that told her that her father would most definitely make a scene if the men clashed. She only hoped they came to a resolution quickly and did not ruin Mr. Benedict's ball.

"I shall tell him you're on the lookout for a husband. He will be well-behaved, I promise. But I'm sure there will be no Waverleys there anyway."

"I wish this feud never existed. It seems so silly arguing over such a small bit of land," Chloe said.

"But it is not just over a bit of land." Her mother took the letter into the drawing room and seated herself at the writing desk, pulling out a fresh sheet of paper with a flourish.

Chloe scurried after and sat on the chaise longue near her mother. "What do you mean *it is not just over a bit of land*? You mean what happened before? With our ancestors?"

Her mother pulled out a quill and dipped it into the inkpot. "No, though goodness knows there has always been bad blood between the families. Even in medieval times they were fighting. Though, I could not tell you about what."

Chloe watched her mother pen the first few lines of the response confirming that they would indeed be attending the ball. "So what else happened?"

Her mother paused and placed the quill back in the pot, turning to face Chloe. "It might seem to you that it is just a silly argument between two old men, but your father has good reasons for disliking Waverley."

"What reasons?" She could not believe that she had been part of this fight for so long and there were other reasons. Reasons that she had been unaware of.

"Well," her mother pressed fingertips to her forehead, "you know that your father was married before me."

Chloe nodded. "She died, did she not?"

"Yes, very young and very quickly. It was quite sad."

"What does that have to do with the Waverleys?"

"Your father married her to save her from the Waverleys. She was pressed into marriage to George and she did not want it one bit. So your father married her instead." Her mother smiled. "Believe it or not, your father was quite the soft character back then. And Waverley has always been an arrogant man. It is no wonder Julia chose your father over him. But, of course, it gave the Waverleys something else to be angry with us about." Her mother sighed. "The worst thing is, your father was looking to repair the relationship back then. They were going to discuss the selling of the land and ensuring no one argued over it ever again. But when your father did the right thing, all civility vanished."

Chloe blinked and blinked again. Her father had his moments, but the story did ring true. She recalled the times when she was a little girl, when he had kissed her grazed knee better or taken her to the library and read to her. Though this argument was making him grumpier with age, she could imagine him coming to the rescue of a woman when he was younger.

Which meant the ongoing argument was all George Waverley's fault, and not her father's. She drew in a long breath. But did that change matters? Did she not still want to put an end to this nonsense? She was not at all sure. Particularly when she was following Mr. Brook Waverley's lead. She had always known him to be a rogue but if his father was so bitter and vile as to try to force a woman into marriage...force her father to play rescuer, well...what sort of son would he produce?

Chloe left her mother to finish penning the reply and retreated to the library. At least there, she could think. Should she continue on with her deal with Mr. Waverley? Should she even trust him? There were so many reasons not to but, well, he had seemed so genuine. She snorted to herself as she shut the library door. She was willing to wager every woman who had fallen for his charms thought him genuine.

"Boo!"

Chloe screamed and whirled to find her brother Freddie tucked at the side of the door.

"At last. I thought you were going to take forever."

She scowled at him and pressed a hand to her racing heart. "Are you trying to kill me?"

He shook his head, vigorously, sending red curls bouncing. He grinned. "No, but it would have been funny if you had fainted." He sauntered over to their father's armchair and sat in it, his legs sprawled over one arm.

"What are you doing in here, anyway?"

"I'm meant to be reading Latin but it's the dullest thing on earth."

Chloe could not argue with that. She plucked up the book from the study desk and leafed through it. "I read this one when I was younger. Do you want me to help?"

"I would rather you throw it in the fire." He lounged back on the chair.

She glanced at the empty fire. "I do not think that would do much good. But you must study." She dragged over another chair and sat at the table, patting the seat. "Come, if we do it together it will go much more quickly."

"Fine." Freddie stood and walked as slowly as possible before flinging himself down onto the chair. She laughed to herself. When Freddie had been born, she thought it the most awful thing. She didn't want a baby around and with him being a boy, she was certain he would get all the attention. Of course, her parents were happy to finally have another baby and for it to be a boy, but it had turned out to be rather fun having a sibling so much younger than herself. It made quite a nice distraction from the trivialities of being an adult woman.

"Papa said if I finished my work, I could ride with him to the border."

"Why would you want to do that?"

"To see if those blasted Waverleys have moved it again." Freddie curled a fist in a manner that reminded her too much of her father.

"Those 'blasted Waverleys' are our neighbors," she said gently.

Freddie lifted both shoulders. "That does not mean they are good people. That is what Papa says."

"Papa...should not say that." Chloe took Freddie's shoulder, forcing him to face her. "One day, this shall be yours..."

Freddie rolled his eyes. "I know, I know."

"No, what I mean is, so shall that disagreement? Do you really wish to spend all your time checking borders and fighting with your neighbors?"

He nibbled on a fingernail, speaking around it, "I don't know." He removed his finger from his mouth. "But what can I do about it?"

Chloe pressed her lips together. Nothing, most likely. At least not yet. But she could. For the sake of her brother and her father, she would have to put her faith in Mr. Waverley. Though, she would guard herself most fiercely against any of his charms. Not that she would expect him to try to use them on her, but it would not do to let her guard down, no matter what.

"Right, let us get to work," she declared, flipping open the book. A little Latin would certainly distract her from the conundrum that was Mr. Waverley.

Hopefully.

Chapter Six

Well, it had worked. Brook allowed himself a smile as the Larkins entered Benedict's ballroom and were announced. He let his smile expand as he took in the sight of Miss Larkin, her curves flattered by a gown that to his rather expert eye was slightly too tight for her. Her red hair was a strawberry swirl piled elegantly on top of her head. He chuckled when he saw her grimace and rub her scalp. No doubt that mass of hair was pinned up tightly and probably hurting her. He could just tell the woman was itching to be out of her gown, dying to pull her hair down and be tucked away amongst books.

As Mr. and Mrs. Larkin glanced around, Brook ducked back behind the dancers. If they spotted him, they would know his father would soon be on his way and no doubt leave immediately. Apparently, Mrs. Larkin had been quizzing Benedict as to who would be in attendance, but they managed to keep the fact that his family would be here from her. He only hoped Benedict did not pay the price for his meddling.

If their fathers resolved their differences, it might be worth it. And Benedict was a big boy, he could handle himself. However, after what his father had told him about Mr. Larkin, he was not sure he would blame his father if he did not wish to resolve the situation.

He slipped around the back of the ballroom, shadowing the Larkins' steps but ensuring he remained out of sight. It was a darn shame that Miss Larkin should come from such poor stock. Did she even realize the bastard her father was? He had to believe not. In his experience, most daughters thought their fathers the best thing in the world, and he doubted she was any different.

Bodies were pressed close together, overpowering floral scents surrounded him, and a woman laughed loudly in his ear. He squeezed through the heaving bodies and pressed a hand through a gap to grab Miss Larkin's hand. She jolted, and he thought he heard the sound of surprise come from her but he could not be certain with the noise and bustle. Twirling, she snatched her hand back, and her annoyed expression did not dissolve as he had expected.

"Come with me," he said to her over the din.

She opened her mouth then closed it. Glancing at her parents, her shoulders dropped a little and she pressed through the crowds to come to his side. "Where are your parents?" She shook her head. "I should have known you would not follow through on your part."

"My father is on his way." Another shrill laugh made him wince. He snatched her hand again and dragged her back toward the entranceway of the ballroom. She tried to remove her hand from his, but he kept a firm grip of her fingers until they were tucked around the corner and away from all the noise.

"That's better." He grinned at her flustered expression.

"Whatever it is you want, talk quickly. I shall not allow myself to be caught with you of all people."

Brook pressed a hand to his heart. "Am I really such a villain?"

"I believe you just might be." She narrowed her gaze at him. "Especially if you are so like your father."

"So like my father?" he echoed.

"I suppose it makes sense you are the way that you are. With such an example to lead you, it is no wonder you think you can take whatever you want, whenever you wish." Miss Larkin rubbed her gloved fingers. "Even my hand."

"I needed to get you away from that crowd. It is impossible to have a conversation in there. Especially with Lady Treadwell laughing in my ear every two seconds."

"Believe it or not, there are better ways to get a lady's attention."

"Oh yes," he said dryly. "I should have simply waved a first edition in your face."

She pursed her lips and cocked her head. "Say whatever it is you wish to say. If your family is not here and have no intention of attending, you could have sent word somehow."

"My family are on their way. No doubt Father's pacing the hallway waiting for my mother as we speak."

"They had better be. If I have attended a ball that I did not need to because you are playing some strange game..."

Brook chuckled. "I am not certain what strange game I could be playing by getting you to attend a ball of all things."

She shrugged, making the jewels on her neck glitter. He could not help but dart his gaze down and eye each little blue stone as they twinkled along her cleavage. He saw the pulse at the base of her neck give a flutter, and he dragged his gaze back up.

"As I said, it is hard to know what to expect from you."

"Ah, yes. Because my father is a bad example." He moved closer, forcing her back into the shadows as more people entered the ballroom, coming past them. She smelled of soap and the tiniest hint of violets. "Pray tell, what exactly do you think he might have done? To be such a bad influence?"

Miss Larkin stared at him for a moment, again her gaze skipping over his expression. "You do not know."

"Know what?"

"Our fathers' argument is about more than just land."

So, she did know. And yet she still took her father's side. It was a pity, because he thought Miss Larkin was cleverer than that. He did not think she would be so blinded by love. Perhaps he had underestimated her.

"I know about that."

"And you have nothing to say on the matter?" she asked. "Really, I should not have even gone along with this plan. I think my father was right about you Waverleys."

"Right?" He scoffed. "I did not have you marked as a fool, Miss Larkin."

"A fool? Because I support my father and his decisions?"

"You really support him after all he has done?" Brook shook his head. "I knew the Larkins were selfish but I had somehow thought you were untouched by it all."

"Selfish? Your father is the very epitome of selfishness." She folded her arms, drawing his attention to her chest. He damned well wished she would stop doing that especially when he was trying to have an argument with her.

"Your father stole *my* father's fiancé. If we are talking of selfishness, I do believe the Larkins win that one."

She gasped. "Stole? My father rescued her. Julia did not wish to be married to such a vile, awful man. My father did his duty and aided her."

He frowned. Brook searched her eyes. She believed that story wholeheartedly. But, the way his father had told it, Marcus Larkin was no savior. Brook released a long breath.

"It seems we have been told different stories about the same matter."

"Different stories?"

He nodded. "Whatever happened between our fathers, they believe it to be different to whatever really happened."

"Your father could be lying about the matter."

"So could yours," he shot back.

"My father is no liar."

"Nor is mine."

"It seems we are at an impasse, Mr. Waverley." She uncrossed her arms. "So what are we to do about it?"

"I think we need to find out what really happened all those years ago. If we are to ever have a hope of repairing the relationship, we need to know."

"I only spoke with my mother. That is how I know what happened. I don't suppose she knows much more. She met my father a few years after this happened."

"I will speak to my mother at some point. Perhaps she knows more. Though, how she will feel about me asking about a previous fiancé, I do not know." He glanced around the side of the doorway. "I think your parents are starting to notice your absence. We had better return."

She nodded. "If I find out anything, how shall I get word to you?"

"Leave me a note at the border. My father will certainly not complain if I check it daily."

Miss Larkin smiled a little and rolled her eyes. "Nor will my father." She stepped out from the shadows. "We had better keep ourselves busy until your father arrives."

Brook tugged out his pocket watch. "My mother is known for being late though I did not expect them to take this long."

"You know how women are, we can never make decisions on what to wear."

"Why do I think that that is not the case with you, Miss Larkin?"

She frowned at him. "I spent quite a while debating what dress to wear tonight, actually."

"I would wager not as long as most women." He grinned. "But you made an excellent choice if that helps."

She blushed and it made his grin expand. "Go on," he urged. "I shall enter in a few moments."

Miss Larkin hurried away, becoming lost in the crowd far too quickly for his liking. He'd rather hoped to watch that curvaceous behind for a few moments more.

She was right, there were differences in their fathers' stories and they needed to find out exactly what had happened. If all this arguing was down to a misunderstanding between the two men, then maybe it could be more easily resolved than they hoped.

He glanced at the doorway. Where the devil was his father, though? It really was not like him to be this late.

Brook headed into the ballroom, aware of a few gazes upon him. It would be impossible to keep his presence from the Larkins forever, so he did not avoid partaking in the ball. He had a few obligatory dances with some young ladies and chatted with several old friends.

He could not help but notice Miss Larkin had not danced once yet. Whether it was because she deliberately avoided dancing or because she had not been asked, he did not know. She sat alone while her parents spoke with friends. It would be a mistake to dance with her. Everyone knew of the rift between the families and they would certainly comment upon them dancing. It might even anger her parents too.

But, damn it, he could not let her sit alone all night. He already knew how much she hated balls.

He strode over, and her eyes widened. "What are you doing?" she hissed. "My parents are watching."

"Let them watch." He lifted a shoulder and offered a hand. "I would like to request the pleasure of the next dance."

"I never dance."

"Tonight you do."

She peered around him, and no doubt there was at least a hundred eyes upon them. Her whole face grew red and finally she stood. "You are impossible," she murmured.

"Indeed I am." He led her onto the dance floor and took up his position. Though he rather regretted that it was a lively country dance and not one where they could be slightly closer. After several reels, he found himself enjoying the sight of her gleaming eyes and wide smile. Despite her protests, Miss Larkin enjoyed dancing.

"For someone who never dances, you danced finely indeed."

"This is a simple dance." She drew a long breath. "Anyone could dance it finely."

He shook his head as he passed by again. "I think you are a secret dancer, Miss Larkin. You likely practice in your bedroom."

"How preposterous, I would never do such a thing."

The way she glanced away from him told differently. He rather enjoyed the image of her prancing around her bedroom in her nightgown. He would not mind viewing such a spectacle in person.

The dance ended all too quickly for his liking. He'd always enjoyed dancing but never quite so much as he had with Miss Larkin. There was something about her innate movements and her ability not to give a fig about what anyone was thinking that made it all the more pleasurable. For a brief moment, he had forgotten why they had joined forces.

He stepped back and bowed to her, and she made a face as she gave a curtsy. Brook chuckled to himself. Perhaps once this was all over, they could actually be friends.

"Mr. Waverley!" Brook turned to find a harried-looking footman dashing toward him. "Mr. Waverley!" The man waved at him. Scowling, Brook made his way through the crowd to meet him.

"What is it?" Tension pooled deep in his stomach. He couldn't think of many reasons why his father would send a footman to fetch him.

"You must return home with haste." The man paused to draw a deep breath. "Your father...your father has taken ill."

"Taken ill?"

"A heart attack I fear. Your mother requests you home at once."

Brook nodded, the dread dissipating and replacing itself with something icy cold. The noise around him dimmed and everything seemed fuzzy.

"Chloe." He peered around for her. He had to tell her he was leaving. That their plan could not take place.

"I am here," she said softly.

She had remained directly behind him and had likely overheard the whole conversation.

"I must go."

She nodded and gave his arm a little squeeze. "I understand. I...I hope everything is well."

At that moment, there was almost nothing he wanted more than to take her in his arms and hold her close. To absorb all the sympathy she radiated. He'd never wanted such a thing from a woman and to want it from the enemy was preposterous. But wanted it, he did.

"Please accept my apologies. I must make haste." He turned to the footman and knocked into someone carrying glasses of wine. One took a tumble and splashed on the front of Miss Larkin's dress. He muttered a curse. "Chloe, damnation. I'm a clumsy fool."

He tugged out a handkerchief and dabbed at the spill on her chest. She batted his hand away. "Go. I can deal with this."

Brook nodded and left her with the handkerchief. Damn it all. He should never have done this. He should never have come to the ball. If he had been at his father's side...

Instead, he had been enjoying himself with Miss Larkin. He only hoped his father never found out.

If he lived, of course.

His father would never forgive him for it.

Chapter Seven

Chloe tilted her head one way, then the other. It was no good—the stain would be there forever. The laundry maid had not been able to remove it and though Chloe had attempted it herself, the stain from the wine that Brook spilled would not budge. She flung the dress aside and landed on her bed in a heap.

She rubbed her dry eyes. The ball had ended late, but even then she had not been able to settle. Her mind whirled over all the things that had happened last night. Though she could not say what she expected to happen at the ball, none of it had been anticipated.

For goodness sakes, she had danced with a Waverley. She was not even sure why she said yes to him only that she could not seem to deny him. She had never been one for finding men in eveningwear appealing, and yet Brook had been devastating in his breeches and finely fitted waistcoat.

Chloe threw herself back on the bed, flinging her arms wide. She landed so her pillows formed a cocoon around her. She flipped around and buried her head into the pillows. What was wrong with her? Why was she wasting so much mental space on Brook Waverley? She could be doing something interesting and important, like finishing her cataloguing of the mythology section in the library or even preparing for Augusta and Joanna to arrive. Neither of them had been able to attend the ball last night, but Joanna promised that they would visit this afternoon.

She supposed one of the benefits of having a widow for a friend was Joanna could play escort to them at any time. Of course, she and Augusta would far rather Joanna's husband was alive. But, as Joanna said, they had to make the best of a bad situation.

Which was what she was doing now, was she not? Making the best of a bad situation? Here she was considering Mr. Waverley in his eveningwear when, for all she knew, his father could be dead. It was highly unlikely her family would find out about it any time soon, so she was left to just wonder. What was he going through? There was a small part of her—no, a rather large part of her—that wished she could be there for him. She had never seen Mr. Waverley look so vulnerable in his life and the way he said her name... Gosh, it rendered her heart still and painful even now.

She had almost thought he might want to fall into her arms that night. If he felt about his father anything like she felt about hers, he would be devastated should anything happen to him.

She rose from the bed and rubbed a hand over her face. There was little she could do about it right now. Perhaps she would go down to the border as he had suggested and leave him a note.

She stood swiftly. Yes, that was an excellent idea. She could do it before Augusta and Joanna arrived and then check tomorrow if there had been any response. She highly doubted there would be. If the house was in mourning, Mr. Waverley would be going nowhere and even if his father was yet alive, she imagined he would not wish to leave his side. But perhaps, just perhaps Mr. Waverley would wish to get some air and see her encouraging note. It was not much, but it was all she could do.

Chloe hastened down the stairs but before she could reach the drawing room to pen a note, her father blocked her entrance. She glanced up at his sour expression. "Whatever is the matter, Papa?"

"I'm surprised you do not know." Her father crossed his arms over his broad chest.

"Papa?"

"Your mother told me not to say anything but it cannot be ignored. You danced with Waverley last night."

"I...I was only being polite. Mother is always telling me to dance more. I would have thought you would have been pleased."

His moustache bristled. "There is no need to be polite to Waverley. You danced with the enemy, Chloe. How do you think that looks?"

"The enemy?" Chloe shook her head. "This is ridiculous, Papa. It was a mere dance with a gentleman."

"You know full well that the Waverley boy is no gentleman. I might not read the gossip columns like you and your mother do, but I am fully aware of his reputation. Do you realize that people were talking of you two last night? There were murmurings of...marriage," he hissed.

"Marriage?" A rush of cold spread through her. She had only danced with him, for goodness sakes. And people knew well of the disagreement between the families. Why would anyone speak of marriage?

"You are of age, Chloe. It is no surprise that anyone you dance with might be assumed to be special to you." His bushy brows lifted. "He is not special to you, is he?"

"I danced with him. Nothing more. How on earth can he be special to me?" Her heart raced. She was a terrible liar, and she was certain her father could see through her. Would he know that she had spent time with Mr. Waverley outside of the ball? Alone?

"If I had known he would have been there, we would never have attended. Let us be grateful that his father was not there or else I would have had to have dragged you away and that truly would have been impolite."

"Father, there is really no need—"

"I never want to hear of you spending time with him again, is that clear?" he demanded.

Chloe searched her father's stern gaze. It was rare he scolded her, especially now that she was a grown woman, but he was utterly serious.

"Chloe?" he prompted.

She nodded solemnly. She could not bring herself to say the words out loud. If Mr. Waverley's father was indeed dead, everything would change anyway. But, there was some small part of her that could not bring herself to promise such a thing. More than anything, she hoped to see him again.

"Where are you off to anyway?"

"I – I was just, um, going to check on the border," she said, aware her voice was turning a little shrill.

"Good. Excellent. I'm glad you are not shirking your duties." Before he could say anything further, Chloe retrieved her coat and gloves and thrust a hat on her head. She hastened out of the house and moved at pace to the border.

Slowing as she reached the border fence, she closed her eyes briefly. In her haste to leave she had not even written the letter. What a fool she was. This whole situation was becoming a disaster. What was she thinking, imagining they could repair the relationship between their fathers? And why was she thinking she could work with Mr. Waverley of all people? He was too handsome, too charming. Not that she wanted to admit that to herself, however, there was no avoiding the matter. She had actually...enjoyed herself last night. She had never enjoyed a ball in her life before.

As she turned around, her gaze caught on a slip of white jammed into a crack in the fence. Surely he had not had time to get a letter to her already? Was he not attending his father's bedside?

Glancing around and feeling ridiculous—for who on earth would be out there spying on her?—she snatched the letter and held it close as she peeled it open. She had never seen Mr. Waverley's handwriting before, but the letter looked rushed.

Her heart gave a little stutter at the words. *Meet me at midnight.*

She stuffed the letter in the pocket of her pelisse and hurried back to the house, her cheeks feeling hot against the cool air outside. She needed to get control of herself before her friends arrived. After all, there was nothing sordid about their meeting. Likely he wanted to update her about his father and perhaps arrange further plans. She had to believe his father was recovering or else he would not be taking the time to leave a letter for her so soon.

So, it was all practically business. Nothing for her to get hot and flustered about.

Even once Augusta and Grace had arrived, heat seemed to linger in her face. She had slipped the letter from her pocket and tucked it into the bodice of her stays. It seemed as safe a place as any, but it made her all too aware of Mr. Waverley's words next to her skin—as though he was somehow touching her.

Joanna gave her a pointed look as they sat down in the drawing room. "Are you quite well, Chloe? You look a little flushed."

"Oh yes." Chloe nodded vigorously. "Quite well. I...I am just a little tired after the ball last night."

"Oh yes, this ball. How did it go?" Joanna asked. "Did you find a library to hide away in?"

"I am not at all sorry I missed out on it." Augusta took a sip of tea. "But I am sorry we were not there for you."

Chloe waved a hand. "Oh, I managed quite well. I even...well, I even danced once."

Augusta choked on her tea. She lowered the cup while Joanna patted her on the back. "You danced?"

Chloe nodded and wondered if she should not have said a word. These were her friends and keeping secrets from them did not sit well but talking of Mr. Waverley made her feel strange and squishy inside.

"Only once," she repeated. "It was for good reason too."

"Was it a handsome man who asked you?" Joanna pressed.

"No. Well, yes. But there was another reason."

Augusta leaned forward. "And are you going to tell us that reason?"

Chloe drew in a long breath and held it for a moment. Why was this so hard? They would understand why she was doing what she was doing. The whole reason she was friends with these two was because they were the least judgmental women she had ever met. They would not be scandalized or tell others of her meetings with Brook.

"It was with Mr. Brook Waverley," she said simply.

"As in the Waverleys with whom your family has a long-standing disagreement?" Joanna's dark eyebrow lifted.

"As in Mr. Brook Waverley, the man you ran away from not so long ago?" Augusta asked.

Sighing, Chloe reached for a slice of fruit cake and took a bite. She was not really hungry, especially for such a rich cake, but she needed a moment to gather herself.

"One and the same," she said after she finished her mouthful. "We have a plan, you see."

"A plan?" Joanna echoed.

"Indeed." Chloe swiftly swiped any crumbs from the corners of her mouth. "We wish to put an end to the argument between our fathers."

Augusta leaned forward. "Exactly whose idea was this?"

"Well, it was Mr. Waverley's," Chloe admitted.

Joanna and Augusta shared a look. Chloe frowned. "What is it?"

"Well, we could not help but notice how he looked at you in the bookshop." Joanna shrugged.

Chloe looked to Augusta, who gave a sheepish smile. "Joanna is not wrong."

"She most certainly is wrong," protested Chloe. "Mr. Brook Waverley has never looked at me with anything but disdain. However, we have decided, for the sake of our families, we must work together."

"And dance together," Augusta said with a smile.

"It was merely so we could talk on what to do," Chloe said primly.

"He is very handsome." Augusta took a nonchalant sip of tea.

Joanna gave a nod of agreement. "And interested in Chloe, I believe."

"His interest begins and ends at fixing the arguments between our family. Nothing more." Chloe lifted her chin. She could not believe her friends thought otherwise. Did they not see a man like Mr. Waverley would never be interested in her? He could have any woman in the world, why would he want of bookish country girl?

And, why on earth did she want to believe that might be true?

Chapter Eight

As he shut the door, Brook pressed a hand to the knot coiled at the top of his spine. He pushed back his shoulders and winced. Really, he should be going to bed, but he doubted he would sleep tonight any more than he did last night. He imagined his mother, who was remaining at his father's bedside, wasn't getting any rest either. Though his father was doing much better, he was frail—frailer than he'd ever seen him before. Brook shuddered. He never wanted to see him like that again.

He looked at the large grandfather clock that stood at the end of the hallway. He had fifteen minutes to get to the border. He would have to make haste or else leave Miss Larkin waiting. Of course, he need not have left her a letter so soon. He doubted she was expecting one and had little idea if she had been to the border today. But he needed to see her.

Because of his father, of course. He had no doubt the strain of this ongoing argument had caused his father's heart attack.

It had nothing to do with wanting to see that smile again. Nothing to do with how he felt strange and empty when he was not in her company. All of that was likely a symptom of having been away from London society for too long, that was all.

Brook walked quickly to the border. There was no way he could ride—he'd had to have disturbed someone and then explained why he was heading out at midnight. The assumption would have been he was off on some assignation—which he was—but not the sort people would assume. The last thing he wanted was for Miss Larkin to get wrapped up in some sort of scandal.

A strange tightness lingered in his throat when he spotted the ghostly outline of her not far from the fence. She had come. He felt the demand of a smile pull at the corners of his lips. It would be the first smile he had issued all day, but he wasn't certain he should be smiling at such a time, so he tamped down the temptation.

She, however, offered one herself. It was hesitant, just curving her full, tempting lips. Behind her eyes, even in the dark, he saw sympathy shining.

"You came," he said as she reached the gate, cursing himself at such an obvious statement.

"Well—" she began at the same time.

Brook paused and motioned for her to continue. Though it was a dark night, Miss Larkin had brought a lantern with her and propped it up on one of the posts. The golden light softened her features and enhanced the red in her hair. Miss Chloe Larkin had never been a traditional beauty and if one analysed her features separately, one would certainly find them wanting in the eyes of many. To him, tonight, she was beautiful.

He closed his eyes briefly. He might want to put an end to this argument between the families, but he did not need to be feeling any...softness toward Miss Larkin. Once they had mended this breach, she would go back to her books and he to London. One night of dancing together did not cancel out their differences, even without the rift between their families.

"How are you? How is your father?" she rushed out.

Aware of the fence dividing them, Brook moved forward to lean his elbows on the wood. He stared briefly out into the darkness, tracing the faint outline of the land ahead of him—land that according to his family was enemy territory. How ridiculous it all seemed that these expanses of fields and wildflowers should be seen as anything other than what they were.

"He is well." He hesitated. "As well as can be expected, at least. He is in recovery and is very frail."

She mimicked him, propping her elbows up on the fence and looking sideways at him. "I am glad to hear he is in recovery, though."

Brook gave a small smile. Her words were genuine even though she really had no reason to offer him such sympathies. They might have joined forces and enjoyed a dance together, but they were far from friends. He had little interest in the argument between the Larkins and Waverleys but he'd never had any interest in Chloe either.

Until now.

But his interest was purely for his father's sake, he reminded himself.

"It gave us all quite a scare," he admitted. "It is always hard to see your parents ageing."

Miss Larkin nodded. "Yes, it is a terrifying thing. I should imagine you—"

"Which is why I think we should push forward with our plans."

"Oh, I was rather thinking you might just want to stop and spend time with your father."

"He shall need some time to rest, but the stress of this disagreement is too much for him. Even this morning he was fretting over the border. We need to put an end to this as soon as we can."

Biting down on her lip, she gave him an uncertain look. "My father is already angry that I spent time with you when we danced. It will not be easy."

"I'm sorry that he is angry with you. Needless to say, last night did not go as I planned."

"It was certainly different to any other ball I have attended," she commented.

"That is probably because you were actually dancing rather than hiding away somewhere," he said dryly.

"Books are far more interesting than people. I still maintain that."

Brook chuckled. "Even more interesting than present company?" He leaned over the fence a little to close the gap between them. "And here I thought you might have enjoyed dancing with me."

She twined her hands together and looked at them. "Well, it was...um...quite enjoyable. I mean, it was satisfactory. Certainly not the worst ball I have ever attended."

"Satisfactory? What high praise," he said with a tilted smile.

He was willing to bet that had it not been for the dark light he would be able to see her blush. She chewed on her bottom lip again.

"Yes, well, anyway, back to the matter at hand. What should we do about our fathers?" she said brusquely.

"Do you have any plans for the next few weeks?"

She shook her head.

"We should meet again and plan more fully. However, we need to get our fathers to neutral land."

"Neutral land? I do not think I could tolerate another ball."

"Come now, it was not so terrible dancing with me."

With a slight tilt of her head, he knew she had conceded.

"I meant actual land. Down by the river where both families' borders end. That is the neutral land that I meant," he explained.

Chloe nodded slowly. "I walk there frequently. It is a peaceful spot."

"Precisely. Hardly the place for an argument." Brook jerked a thumb in the direction of the spot. "There neither of them can get angry over the other being on their land."

"They can still get angry, though."

"Which is why we shall be there to be the voices of reason. I can be walking with my father and you can be walking with yours. My father has been told that he needs fresh air once he is up and about. It will be a fine excuse."

"My father and I walk together quite frequently so it will not seem strange to ask."

"Excellent." Brook straightened, pushing away from the fence. "We should meet again, to finalize when we shall do this. My father shall need a little time to recover first."

"I shall check for your letters whenever I can."

He wasn't certain why but the idea of Miss Larkin anxiously awaiting his letter made his heart feel a little warm. They could confirm the plans over letters really, but he wanted to see her again.

There, he had admitted it to himself. He was beginning to rather like Miss Chloe Larkin's company.

"You had better return home before you are missed," he said.

She shrugged. "My parents are heavy sleepers, they shall not know I am gone. Besides, I am known to be still reading at this time of night. They probably think I'm in the library."

"Of course you are." And now he was struck with the desire to sneak into her house and watch her read, curled up by a fire in her shift, her hair all loose around her shoulders. It had to be the most mundane of imaginings he had ever had and yet it was all too appealing.

"Shall I walk you back?" His voice came out a little raspy.

"I shall be safe enough. The worst that will happen is that I step in sheep droppings. And it would be far more dangerous to be walking with you."

"I hope that you are saying that because of our fathers' disagreement and not because you really believe I am a danger to your person."

She pushed away from the fence and gave a little smile. "You are a rake, Mr. Waverley, everyone knows it. My reputation would be well and truly sullied if we were spotted alone."

"Ah, yes, a rake. I forgot." He rolled his eyes. "I did not realise someone with your reading repertoire would be interested in the gossip columns."

"I know full well the columns are prone to exaggeration, but there is always a grain of truth to every rumour. You have never denied your reputation before, Mr. Larkin, so I am not certain as to why you are doing it now."

No, nor was he. The talk surrounding his activities had never bothered him before. He enjoyed life to the fullest and made no apologies for it. Silly, stilted rules of society could go hang as far as he was concerned.

"Well, this rake had better bid you adieu. I would not wish to scare away any future suitors with my presence."

She narrowed her gaze at him. "You know full well there are no future suitors."

"Perhaps if you got your nose out of the book, you would find a few more."

"Now you're starting to sound like my mother." She folded her arms. "How terribly dull."

"Forgive me. I promise to never, ever sound like a mother again."

"And will you promise not to tease me again?"

"That, I cannot do. You, Miss Larkin, are far too much fun to tease. I especially like it when you get that frustrated expression...yes, there it is right now."

She blew out a breath and uncrossed her arms. "You really are impossible. How we are to ever work together, I do not know."

"We shall manage just fine. For our fathers' sake, we must."

Her shoulders dropped a little. "Yes, you're right. And, Brook, I really do wish your father a full recovery." She leaned over and touched his arm briefly.

Brook stilled at the touch, regretting that it was so brief. His father's ill-fortune was quickly forgotten, but now it struck with full force. And now he wanted to vault over the fence and wrap her in his arms, to absorb every ounce of comfort she could give him.

Instead, he dipped his head. "I shall send word soon."

"I shall be waiting."

Waiting. Waiting for him. Good Lord, why did he like that far too much?

Chapter Nine

She really ought to cease the pacing. If her father saw her like this, he would figure out something was wrong. Chloe's father was no simple man and, unfortunately, he knew his daughter too well. There really was no need for all the pacing, after all. She and Brook had a plan. What was the worst that could happen?

She grimaced to herself. The two men could get in a fight, she admitted to herself. What sort of fight either of them could put up, she did not know, but she suspected out of stubbornness both men would do an injury to themselves.

But her father was a reasonable man, really he was. It was only about the border matter did he ever get so angry. He clearly believed he was very much in the right but neither she nor Brook could figure out whose story was correct. Her own mother refused to talk about it, waving a hand and telling her she was tired of the matter. It was hardly something she could press the local farmers about, either. It was certainly not the done thing to discuss any family matters with them.

Though, there were a few tenant farmers who had been on the land nearly forty years. They would be the people who would know something.

She nibbled on the end of her thumb and glanced out of the drawing room window. The weather was fine and bright, a few clouds dotted the sky, but no wind touched the trees today, unlike yesterday. They had, it seemed, chosen the perfect day to trick their fathers into meeting.

Oh Lord, there went those nerves again. That strange, swirling uncomfortable sensation rioted around her stomach and made her feel hot and prickly. She took a moment to draw in a long breath and exhale it slowly. Alas, the sensations did not subside, and a small voice in the back of her mind jabbed at her. It was not just the idea of their fathers meeting that did this to her.

No, it was seeing Brook again.

Oh yes, he had become Brook in her mind. Whether she was Chloe to him yet, she did not know, but she could not wait to find out.

He had managed to meet once on the border in the last week so they could finalize their plans. Of course, she had found herself down by the fence nearly every day, waiting for one of his letters. It was an easy enough scenario to plan, both fathers liked the outdoors and with Brook's father on the road to recovery, it made sense for him to take some fresh air. However, their letters had turned swiftly away from planning this event to something else. Something she had never done before.

If she wrote to her friends, her letters were friendly and informative. If she wrote to relatives, she would tell them the news and stick to formalities. But the letters with Brook... Well, they were different. Whenever she put quill to paper to write to him, she found herself divulging all manner of matters. And he would of course tease her in the letter in return and she would be forced to scold him most readily.

Without even realizing it, a smile spread across her face. For some ridiculous reason, she rather liked his teasing. She suspected he rather liked her scolding too.

Shaking her head to herself, she moved into the main hall-way and cocked her head to listen for her father's footsteps. They came slowly, followed by the light tap of the cane. Her father's knee was bothering him with the ever-changing weather, and she was not at all sure she should still be insisting on this walk, but her father refused to admit that he was in too much pain to do such a thing. The man would likely drag himself there out of spite if she insisted on remaining home.

She watched him come downstairs, his features a careful mask, but she could see the slight wince behind his eyes with each step. Blast, perhaps she should have cancelled. There had to be some other way to get their fathers to meet, surely?

"Are you certain you want to go out today?" she asked. "It looks like it might...rain."

"Rain?" her father scoffed. "There is nary a cloud in the sky, girl."

"I know, Papa, but..." She could not bring herself to tell him he was too frail to do a mere walk.

He waved a hand. "You asked me if I would like to accompany you on a walk, and goodness knows, you do not spend enough time out of doors. It would be remiss of me indeed to cancel on you." He smiled warmly. "Of course, it is rare for a father to get time alone with his daughter when she is an adult. I will confess to looking forward to it."

Oh, Chloe did not know whether to feel guilty or warmed by the sentiment. What he was picturing as a pleasant afternoon out, was going to turn something very much the opposite. However, his kind words reminded her of the man behind all the frustration about the border matter. He might command her never to see Brook and get angry and demand that she go check on the border far too often, but he was still her father, and he loved her very much. She loved him equally as much and that is why this feud had to end. He could not live out his last days so infuriated by such a matter.

"Well, what are we waiting for?" her father asked.

Giving herself a mental shake, Chloe looped her arm through her father's offered one. They moved at a slow pace, following the path away from the house until it reached the riverside. Water flowed swiftly, clear enough for her to see minnows and sparkling rocks beneath. They took a left and followed the natural path leading through the trees and along the riverside. Though wide, it was a shallow river and she had spent many a day as a child dipping her feet in it or sitting on the riverbank and reading a book. Those had been the times before she'd been aware there was even an argument between the two families. Perhaps if she was careful, she could probe her father on the matter.

"Papa," she began.

His face contorted, and he inhaled sharply. As she turned to him, he tried to hide his pained expression, but she caught it just in time.

Unlooping her arm from his, she tilted her head and eyed him. "Papa..."

He sighed. "Perhaps I had better rest for a moment." He pointed to a tree with his cane. "That looks like an excellent sitting spot."

She bit on her lip while her father settled himself down against the tree. She would need to get word to Brook that they could not come or that he and his father needed to travel further. That would bring them onto Larkin land, however, which could certainly be dangerous indeed. Even in her father's state. Oh dear, what to do?

"Do not be downhearted, Daughter. Why do you not go on without me? I know how much you enjoy your walks by the river. You can come back for me and we shall walk the rest of the way home."

"But, Papa..."

He shook his cane at her. "Go on, I insist. I shall enjoy the fresh air and the peace for a while." He yawned. "This looks like the perfect spot for a little nap."

Chloe grimaced. There was no persuading him but as his knee was painful, she did not wish to. Nor did she wish to leave Brook waiting for her, so she had better make haste. Giving her father a quick peck on the cheek, she continued along the path until it started to open into a clearing.

Her pulse began to speed up when she spotted the broad shoulders and long legs of Brook. She frowned. But no Mr. Waverley. It seemed neither of them had managed to bring their father along.

"Brook?"

He turned swiftly, and his expression softened when it landed on her. He glanced left and right. "No father?"

She shook her head. "No. And you do not have one either?"

"No. But I do have a mother." He jerked his head to the right of him. "She is admiring some flowers not far from here. She shall return before long. My father was not feeling well enough, but I did not want to leave you waiting here alone. Unfortunately, my mother decided she wanted to walk instead."

"Ah. My father made it some of the way, but his knee is causing him problems at the moment."

"It seems we really are destined never to get our fathers together."

Chloe closed the gap between them and pressed a hand to his arm. "We shall just have to keep trying. It was a good plan," she insisted.

He gave her a half-smile. "You are a stubborn woman, are you not?"

She nodded vigorously. "The stubbornest." She grinned.

There was a rustle from the trees and the sound of a woman humming. "That's my mother. I do not know how she will react to your presence, but I think it best that she does not see us together. She will suspect something is up."

"Oh yes. I shall tuck myself in those trees over there and wait until you are gone." She thrust a thumb in the direction of a group of trees by the riverside. She had squeezed herself between them many times as a child and they made an excellent hiding spot.

He nodded. "Let us meet again soon."

"Of course." As she hurried away to hide herself, she tried to shoo away the silly, excited feeling in her stomach. Brook wanted to see more of her. How foolish she was. It was only because of his determination to fix the rift between their families. Nothing more.

She squeezed herself in between the trees, wincing as the branches pressed into her stomach and breasts. She rolled her eyes at herself. The last time she had hidden here, she had probably been a darned sight smaller. She would be lucky if she could get out.

She peered through the leaves, satisfied that she was well hidden from Brook's mother. His mother emerged, holding a bunch of flowers. She could not quite make out what they were saying, but they conversed briefly and his mother left. Brook watched her leave then headed toward her position. "You can come out now."

Chloe gave a little wriggle. Oh dear Lord. She was stuck fast. "Oh no, you go ahead. I shall just...stay here for a moment."

"I made an excuse to remain. Now we can discuss our next steps rather than sneaking out of the house during the night again."

She wriggled again, but the branches seemed to press harder into her skin. There was no way of disentangling herself from this with any chance of being ladylike. Brook would never let her forget it.

"I...I think I quite like it in here. I might just remain here a little while."

Brook came closer, his brow creasing. "Chloe, are you, by any chance, stuck?"

She let her head drop, and heat flowed into her cheeks.

"Chloe?"

"Fine. It is because I am far too plump for this hiding spot anymore. And I am completely and utterly stuck. Happy now?"

His lips tipped. "You are certainly far too well-endowed to hide in there. Though, I would not normally say such endowment is a bad thing, you are perhaps not made to hide between trees."

She huffed. Could he make this anymore worse?

"Give me your hand." He thrust a hand between the branches toward her.

She weighed her options. She could remain and he would probably remain with her, teasing. Or she could continue to try to tear herself out and do herself an injury. And probably ruin yet another dress. Or she could swallow her pride and take his hand.

She supposed the latter was the better option. Reluctantly, she slipped her hand into his, aware of their gloves brushing against one another. His strong, capable fingers wrapped around hers then he offered his other hand, and she took that as she wriggled from side to side while he pulled.

Slowly but surely, she emerged from between the branches. When the last branch gave way, she popped out like a cork from champagne and stumbled forward, launching them both back toward the river. He caught her in his arms, but it was too late. Her weight upon him forced him backward and they toppled into the shallows by the river.

"Oh no." Cold water splashed up her hems and soaked through her layers. She landed fully atop him, her hands upon his chest. The river lapped at the sides of his jacket.

Dropping her head down, she rested her forehead against his chest. It was not making the situation any better, but she was not sure she could bear to look at him. What a fool she had made of herself.

His body shook, and she knew she should move. No doubt he was freezing in this water. It took her a moment to realize the shaking was coming from laughter. She lifted her head and stared at him. "What is so funny?"

"This." He splashed his hands into the river. "Somehow, being with you has turned into quite an adventure, Chloe."

She looked at his amused expression and felt a tiny smile of her own slip across her lips. It *was* a rather ridiculous situation to get into.

He gripped her arms and eased her off him, then helped her to her feet. It was only then did she become aware that she had been pressed fully against him, feeling every hard ridge of his thighs and the rise and fall of his chest as he breathed. Any chill from the river swiftly dissipated, and she glanced away from him.

Brook pressed a finger under her chin to force her to look at him. "Are you hurt, Chloe?"

She shook her head. "Only my pride."

"At least it was only I who witnessed it."

"You are probably the worst person to witness it. You shall be retelling this story forever."

He lifted a shoulder. "Perhaps. But I shall tell it with fondness."

He glanced down at his soggy breeches and her soaked hems. "We should dry off before returning home. I am not certain how either of us shall explain this."

Chloe considered her father waiting for her but suspected he had most likely settled in for an afternoon nap. He would not miss her.

"Yes, you're right," she agreed, despite the fact that her family would quite readily accept that she had been silly and slipped in. And if Brook's parents were still questioning him at his age, that would be a curious thing indeed. Whatever the reason for insisting they spend more time together, she could not bring herself to argue against it.

"Come with me." He took her hand as though that was the most natural thing in the world. It did not even feel strange to slip her fingers in his, though it did make her stomach punch and her breath feel a little shaky. He led her out of the woods and into the fields, following a path that she had never taken before until they merged out onto a sunny spot of land that was free from the shade of trees or the view of farmhouses and buildings.

"This is another of my favorite spots," he explained.

"I am on Waverley land here, am I not?"

"You are. You should not be discovered. No one comes here except me."

Chloe pursed her lips. "So I'm on enemy territory. Should I be concerned for my welfare?"

"I think you're more likely to get yourself into trouble without my help."

"Perhaps," she conceded.

Slipping off his jacket, he laid it on the grass and motioned for her to sit. He sat beside her and pushed up his shirtsleeves. She glanced at his forearms which were lightly dusted with hair and his veins flexed as he moved his fingers. She had never studied a man's arms before but Brook's were infinitely fascinating for some reason.

She glanced away when he looked toward her. Hopefully he had not noticed her interest. She was all too aware that this man held all the power. He was known for being a charmer and a rake and she was known for...well liking books. And now for being clumsy. The last thing she needed was for him to think she was interested in him.

"Relax, Chloe, we shall not be discovered."

He laid back, his hands behind his head and his eyes drifted closed. She stole the quickest of peeks at his profile, at the way his thick lashes fell against his skin. His lips, when relaxed, begged for the touch of fingers. It was no wonder he had so much success with women, he was like a work of art.

Shaking her head at herself, she followed his suit and laid back, letting the sun prickle its way along her skin and begin to dry her. She would have to be far more cautious and cease any silly thoughts toward Brook. He might look like a harmless, sleeping man, but he was dangerous. In every way.

Chapter Ten

"Will you cease looking at me so?"

Brook's expression remained neutral. His father laid down his newspaper and glowered at him. "I have had enough of your mother looking at me like that, I do not need it from you too." His father waved a hand. "Do you not have something to do? Some ladies to charm perhaps?"

Brook nearly snorted. He had not charmed a lady in weeks, not since he started plotting with Chloe. He did not think she was charmed so she certainly did not count.

"Perhaps I'm simply enjoying your company, Father." He sank onto the chair next to his father's which faced the fireplace in the study. There was no fire as it was too warm, but they had a habit of convening there whenever he was home and mulling over the world or sometimes simply sitting in silence. Though he preferred the hubbub of London, he did relish the moments with his father. He hoped for many more of them.

It would not happen if they did not bring an end to this disagreement between the families as soon as possible. Even in his father's current state, he was still demanding people go and check the border and letting himself get far too angry about the matter.

The problem was, he had not come up with anything new as yet. If they could not arrange a simple walk, what else could they do?

Brook allowed himself a small smile. At least it meant he could keep exchanging letters with Chloe. All her time spent with her nose in books meant she was a talented wordsmith and there was something quite delightful about parrying words with her, even through the form of the written word. If someone had told him he would enjoy letter writing a few months ago, he would have laughed in their face. But, then, there was little to entertain in the countryside so he had to get it where he could find it.

He tapped his fingers on the arm of the chair. He and Chloe needed to meet again soon. He hoped at least the midnight meetings ensured they would never be caught. A rake he might be, the last thing he wanted to do was harm Chloe.

"I am tired, Brook," his father said on a heavy breath.

"Shall I take you upstairs?" Brook began to rise from the chair, but his father indicated for him to sit.

"That is not what I meant. I'm tired of people treating me as though I am in my grave. This little...event"—he waved a hand—"may have knocked the wind from me for a little while but it is not the end of me, Brook." His father jabbed a finger in his direction. "Trust me on this, it is not the end of me."

"No one thinks that it is—" Brook began.

"That's a damned lie," his father spat. "Even my solicitor wanted to discuss my will, should anything happen. I told that bastard I am happy with it the way it is."

"Father..."

"Promise me you will stop feeling sorry for me," he ordered. "Even if these are my last days—which they are not—I would want us to behave as we have always done. None of this pandering to me and tiptoeing around. You hear me, lad? I will have no more of it."

Brook chuckled. "Very well. If that is what you wish."

"It is what I wish." His father thumped a fist down on the arm of his chair. "Now get your rear out of this house and go do something interesting. You and I both know this is the most amount of time you have ever spent here without doing anything. I insist you go and find some lovely ladies to charm or a friend to have a drink with."

"Perhaps I do not wish to have a drink, Father. Have you thought of that? And there are few ladies in the area to charm."

"That's a lie."

"Well, perhaps I have already charmed them all and there are none left."

"That sounds about right." His father gave an amused snort. "Well, whatever you do, make it interesting."

Brook rose from the chair. "As you wish, Father. Should I get into any trouble, I shall blame you thoroughly."

"Good. I should like to be the cause of some trouble."

Chuckling to himself, Brook left the study, though he hardly had an inkling of an idea as to what he was going to do. He could visit Benedict but the man was still thoroughly in love with his wife and Brook always felt like he was encroaching. Several of his friends were in London and many others in Bath. He had intended to join them were it not for his father's illness. He had somehow expected to reunite the two families within a matter of weeks and be done with it, then he could be off celebrating with friends.

He had to admit to himself it was a rather foolish thought to think that centuries of hate between the two families could be healed within weeks.

Dressing for the outdoors, Brook ambled outside. His mother was out visiting, and it was times like this he regretted not having a sibling or two. This was one of the main reasons he did not much enjoy spending a lot of time in Hampshire—there was simply not enough entertainment. He imagined Chloe would beg to differ and scold him for being childish.

With that thought in mind, he cut through the rock garden, following the path that sliced between the carefully curated plants until he exited the other end. Once there, another path meandered up a slope for a while before leading to the edge of the formal land. Now he was onto the wild fields that would take him to the river...and the fence.

He should not even be bothering. He'd only left her a letter yesterday and he doubted she'd found time to reply so quickly, but at least it was something to do. Maybe...just maybe she would be there. Gads, what had happened to him? Chasing after a piece of skirt for no more than a letter?

Despite feeling a fool, he made his way to the fence to find no letter and no sign of Chloe. As he had expected. It did not mean his heart did not sink. Leaning briefly against the fence, he rested his jaw upon his hands. What should he do now?

He straightened at the sight of something. Or someone. Definitely female, with a parasol shielding her face. It had to be Chloe, surely? Who else would it be?

"Chloe!" He lifted a hand.

She turned toward him, and his heart dropped low into his stomach down to his toes. It was most certainly not Chloe.

It was her mother.

Damn, he had given away their acquaintance. Chloe really would have something to scold him about now. He glanced around and debated his next move. He could run or pretend he had not seen her, though neither move would exactly improve his standing in her mother's eyes. If they were ever to mend the relationship between the families, he would hope to be civil with her too.

He sighed. There was nothing he could do but try to explain away why he had called Chloe's name. He straightened as Mrs. Larkin neared and gave a courteous nod. She looked so like an older version of Chloe, with ashy strawberry hair and a full figure, that it was almost eerie. "Mrs. Larkin."

"Mr. Waverley." She peered at him from under her hat, tilting back the parasol to look him up and down. "Whatever are doing out here?"

"Oh just...uh..."—he kicked the fence—"checking the boundaries."

"I see." She narrowed her gaze. "As you can see, they are not yet moved."

"Yes, yes I can see that. Excellent." He cleared his throat. "Well, I shall be—"

"Mr. Waverley," she called before he could turn away.

"Yes, ma'am?"

"Why exactly did you call me daughter's name?"

"Your daughter's name?" He shook his head vigorously. "I believe you are mistaken, m—"

"If you are trying to call me old and of poor hearing, I should watch your tongue, Mr. Waverley."

Brook had to resist a smile. So that was where Chloe got her fire from. "Forgive me."

"Tell me the truth now. I saw you two dancing together at Mr. Benedict's ball and Chloe never dances with anyone. Would you say you are acquainted?"

He clasped his hands behind his back. He could not lie to her, but he could hardly tell her the truth either. From what Chloe said, her mother would not be happy about them interfering in their fathers' business.

He nodded slowly. "Yes, we are acquainted."

"Well, that explains my daughter's demeanor of late." She pursed her lips. "I hope you understand that Chloe is naïve but far cleverer than either of us. I trust her not to make a fool of herself. I hope I can trust you to be a gentleman."

"You can, ma'am. I swear it."

"Very well. We shall say nothing more on it."

"Mrs. Waverley...uh...is Chloe at home today?" He spilled out the question before he had thought it through properly.

The hint of a smile curved the woman's mouth. "She is not. And even if she was, you would certainly not be welcome there, Mr. Waverley."

"Ah. Of course. Yes—"

"She is in the village with her friends. No doubt she shall be visiting the bookshop," Chloe's mother said airily.

"I—" Before he could thank her, she turned and headed away from the fence.

Brook watched her leave then let his shoulders drop and unclasped his hands. He peered at the back of his hands. Nail marks were etched into the back of them. He needed to be much, much more careful. If that had been Mr. Larkin, he'd likely have a bullet in him or be facing a duel.

Still, he quite fancied a stroll into the village. After all, nothing could be said if he just happened to be in the same shop as Chloe. He grinned to himself. He was as entitled to browse for books as the next man.

Chapter Eleven

"You two go on without me," Chloe suggested, shooing Joanna and Augusta toward the door. "I shall be some time longer, I am sure."

Augusta tipped her head. "Are you certain? I really do not think—"

Joanna tapped on Augusta's arm. "If she does not need us here, I suggest we go. We will meet you at the haberdashery."

"Yes, please do. I shall see you there." Chloe gave them a smile. Her friends, even though well-read, could not match her passion for books and her ability to browse for hours on end. She would rather explore the shop alone, even though she had likely looked upon every single book that was here by now.

Once her friends were gone, Chloe moved back into the depths of the shop. Here were the older titles, some looking neglected and slightly covered in dust. She had a fondness for these and had been known to purchase one or two frequently. She could not help but feel sorry for these books, outshone by the newer titles that everyone was clamoring to read.

"I should have known I would find you here." Chloe snapped her head up at the sound of those deep timbres that made her want to release a little shiver.

"Brook." His name came out a raspy whisper.

He smiled broadly, making her stomach do a little flip.

"Whatever are you doing here?"

"I shall confess to hoping to find you here." He picked up a book and leafed through it nonchalantly before snapping it shut and placing it back upon an unsteady pile.

Chloe glanced around the alcove. They were out of sight of the shopkeeper and there was only one other customer near the front. Chloe edged deeper into the recesses of the shop, letting the gloom of the windowless room swallow her.

"I know you have your reputation to consider but one can hardly get into trouble for browsing books in the same shop as me." He stalked her steps, closing the gap between them again.

"One can get in trouble if one is fraternizing with the enemy," she pointed out.

His lips tilted. "I had rather hoped you would stop thinking of me as the enemy."

She glanced over him. "I'm not yet certain what you are."

"A friend, perhaps."

She could feel her defenses weakening. It always happened around Brook. Perhaps it was his charming smile or the way he spoke to her as though she were an equal. Whatever it was, she was unable to barricade herself against him. The smile she had been fighting quirked the corners of her lips.

She lowered her voice. "I'm not certain midnight meetings count as friendship."

"Most people would consider that an illicit liaison. I should imagine you would rather think of those as a meeting between two friends."

She opened her mouth then closed it. An illicit liaison? Of course, she was not foolish enough to imagine that people would think there were good intentions behind their meetings.

However, she would not have thought Brook would think to mention meetings with her and *illicit liaisons* in one breath. After all, she was hardly the sort of person anyone had *illicit* anythings with.

"If...that is...you could have sent me a message if you wanted to meet." Chloe twisted to eye the books in front of her, anything to remove her gaze from Brook, who was looking at her with that dangerously devilish smile and that glint in his eyes.

The man was teasing her and, damn him, it was working. She was feeling all hot and prickly, and her mind kept darting back to the idea of this illicit liaison. She could not help but wonder, what would it be like to meet with Brook for such a thing? How would he charm her? What would he do? It was not something a girl like her could ever have considered.

But here she was, considering such a thing. She blew out a long, slow breath she hoped he could not hear or else he might catch the shuddery quality.

He moved to her side, leaning against the pale brick pillar that supported the ceiling of the shop. She glanced at him from the periphery of her vision then forced her gaze to the titles on the spines. All the words and letters seemed to blur together as she made a show of reading each one as if they meant something to her.

"We do need to discuss trying to arrange another meeting," he said.

"As I said, you could have sent me a message." She tugged out a random book, flicked through it and pretended to be absorbed in the words.

Brook plucked the book from her hand and eased it shut. "I wanted to see you sooner than that."

Her gaze snapped to his. Blast. He was winning. She could not help herself, finding her attention drawn into his eyes where all sorts of sense vanished.

"Why...why should you wish to see me sooner?" She shouldn't have asked. It did not matter. He was likely simply keen to come up with another plan. Just because she enjoyed his company, did not mean he felt the same way.

He did not answer for a moment. Something odd flickered in his gaze before vanishing behind that charming grin.

"If you wish to discuss our fathers meeting, I could think of better places to do it," she said hastily. "Plenty of my father's friends frequent here. In fact, I think I saw Mr. Johnson heading this way earlier. And of course Mr. Bramley knows my father well. He shall report back to him if he sees us together. I really do think—"

"Chloe."

She clamped her lips together. She was rambling like a fool and it was all because she was standing in one square foot with Brook Waverley, known rake, and a man entirely in another league to her.

"Is it so hard to believe that I might actually wish to spend time with you? And, given our parents' disagreement, I could never do that in the traditional manner."

"But—" She scowled.

There was no hint of charm or guile in his words. In fact, he seemed almost frustrated that she might think he had other motives. Before she could come up with a reply, the bell on the front door jangled. She peered toward the front of the shop and sucked in a breath. "It's Mr. Johnson," she gasped. Though she had been talking nonsense, Mr. Johnson was indeed one of her father's close friends and one who could be considered on the 'Larkin side'. He would surely tell her father if he spotted her with Brook.

Brook grasped her arm and dragged her deep into the recesses of the building. A small door leading to what was likely a storage room was tucked between shelves of books. She had seen the shopkeeper come in and out with new books from there. Brook turned the handle and tucked her in, shutting the door behind them.

Darkness enveloped them, and she could not tell how big the room was. Given Brook's proximity, she suspected it was small indeed, no larger than a cupboard.

"We cannot stay here all day," she whispered.

"I could think of worse ways to spend my day."

"Well—"

Brook pressed fingers to her lips at the sound of voices nearing. She stilled, recognizing the voice of Mr. Johnson and the shopkeeper.

"Oh Lord." Surely they did not need to come in the room? If they did, Chloe would be utterly ruined, and she certainly would not expect Brook to step in and do the right thing.

She frowned to herself in the darkness. Would she? He was charming and certainly roguish but the more she came to know him, the more she had begun to wonder—was he really the rake that she had read about in the gossip columns?

What silly thoughts these were. Brook would never marry someone like her! Goodness, Mr. Brook Waverley would likely never marry at all or have some clever arrangement to ensure that he still had his freedom as well as heirs.

Her throat grew dry, and she fought the urge to cough. The air in the storage room was dusty and smelled of dry paper. Only the scent of soap coming from Brook broke through it. Fighting the desire to inhale that smell deeply was difficult indeed, especially when it would most certainly bring on a coughing fit.

The voices faded and she released the air from her lungs. It was only then that she realised that Brook had her by both arms and they were mere inches apart. Instead of slowing, the heart beat that pounded fiercely in her ears grew more voracious.

Though she could not make out his features, she felt as though his gaze was upon her. She longed to be in the sunlight, able to see what was in his eyes. But would she even see what she wanted? She licked her lips. "Brook..." she whispered.

His fingers came back to her mouth but not to shush her this time. No, this time he traced the shape of her lips and let that finger slip down, over her chin and down her neck to where she could feel her pulse beat wildly. His fingers curved fully around her neck, pushing under her hair while his other hand felt warm on her arm, as though his fingers were on fire and penetrating through all layers of her clothing.

She waited, lips parted. She might be ignorant in the ways of men in the world, but she was not wrong about this, was she? There was only one reason a man might take a woman in his arms like this.

And for the life of her, she could not find any reason for him not to kiss her.

"Chloe," he murmured, his tone almost as raspy as hers had been. The sound of her name on his lips sent the tiny hairs on her arms standing on end.

She leaned into him—her way of telling him, *yes, I want this too.*

He must have understood her. Somehow, by some miracle, this roguish man actually understood her—the bookish recluse whom everyone was more than happy to ignore.

His lips upon hers came as a shock and she jolted. He dropped back. "Forgive me."

"No, please...I mean..." Curses, he had taken her shock for refusal. "Kiss me, Brook."

He chuckled likely because her tone was demanding. She had not meant to be, but she needed this more than she had ever needed anything in her life. Even if it was only one kiss, it would be one kiss to carry her through the rest of her spinsterhood.

She waited what felt like an eternity in the darkness but must have been mere seconds. His lips touched hers tentatively, and she managed to remain still. They were warm and seeking, moving across her mouth with expert tenderness. Chloe remained with her hands balled into fists at her sides. The riot of sensation rolled through her and her mind froze. Gone were the questions as to why and how this would happen.

He kissed her again, curving his thumb up her jawline and gently angling her head. He broke away briefly, resting his forehead against hers. "Chloe, you can kiss me back, you know."

"I do not know how," she blurted out.

She half expected him to laugh at her but instead he released her arm and cupped the other side of her face. Gently, slowly, he helped her move, helped her participate in the kiss until her knees felt weak and she was not even sure whether up was up and down was down. Slowly, she unfurled her fists and put her hands to his waist. She felt warmth and strength underneath his jacket, and it made her heart all fluttery.

Brook eased away, pressing one firm kiss to her lips, then to the tip of her nose. He kept ahold of her face, and she felt his warm breath on her skin.

"You have never been kissed before?"

She shook her head, even though she knew he could not see but he must have felt it.

"Well, I am honored to be your first."

Somehow, she did not melt into a puddle at his feet. Though it was close. He had said those words with utter sincerity and she genuinely believed them to be true. Good Lord, what a muddle she was in.

Chapter Twelve

"Mr. Waverley, what an unexpected pleasure!" Mrs. Joanna Lockhart had a smile on her face that passed for mischievous. Between her and another girl whom Brook could not remember the name of, was Chloe. Her cheeks were still flushed from the kiss. She had insisted on leaving the bookshop before him and catching up with her friends. She was not wrong to do so but he'd be damned if he wanted to break from her company so soon.

"Mrs. Lockhart." He bowed his head. "And Miss Larkin and..."

"Miss Snow," the petite dark-haired girl said softly, dipping to him.

"We were just walking back to my carriage. Will you not join us for a moment?" Mrs. Lockhart asked.

Brook did not miss the look Chloe shot her friend's way but Mrs. Lockhart ignored it as did Brook when it was darted his way. "I would be delighted."

Brook inserted himself into the gap between Mrs. Lockhart and Chloe and they strolled along the main road that cut through the village, leading straight between the scattered shops—a chandlery, the old forge, a tea shop, and an odds and ends shop. Some medieval buildings remained, their white-washed walls contrasting with the more modern red brick structures. The road leading between them all was not paved and large ruts cut a groove through it from the many carriages that passed through daily.

"I am surprised to see you here, Mr. Waverley," Mrs. Lockhart commented.

"Oh, why is that?" he asked nonchalantly. The attractive woman gave him an appraising look. He could not say what Chloe had told them about their acquaintance, but it was apparent she was interested in him—and not for herself. He rather liked that Chloe had a protector in this friend.

"You are normally in London at this time of year, are you not? Or Bath? I believe that is where the most...*fun* is to be had."

"Mr. Waverley's father has fallen ill, remember, Joanna?" Chloe said quietly.

"Oh yes. Are you remaining to nurse him back to health? Or is there someone else keeping you here?" Mrs. Lockhart's smile tilted.

"I am, of course, concerned for my father," he replied, keeping his expression neutral.

"And there is no other reason for you to remain?" Mrs. Lockhart pressed.

"Joanna," Chloe hissed.

"There are several reasons for me to remain in Hampshire. After all, there are many wonderful people here—much like yourself, Mrs. Lockhart." He shot her a bold smile.

They came to a stop by the fountain at the end of the town. The one cobbled section allowed carriages to circle around and collect passengers. Two empty hacks awaited passengers and a small private one that he assumed belonged to Mrs. Lockhart's family was tucked behind them.

"Spoken like a true gentleman." Mrs. Lockhart eyed him. "I hope you are a true gentleman, Mr. Waverley. I would so hope for all those stories of you not to be true."

He met her gaze firmly. "I was not aware you read stories such as those, Mrs. Lockhart. I am certain you are aware such stories are greatly exaggerated and I would never cause harm to any woman's reputation."

A moment passed and the woman nodded. She leaned in a little and dropped her voice. "If you ever cause hurt to my friend, I shall ensure that you never touch another woman again."

Brook chuckled. "I believe you wholeheartedly."

"Good." She affected a pleasant smile. "Well, it was wonderful to see you, Mr. Waverley. Will you be walking Chloe home? You are neighbors after all."

"But—"Chloe spluttered.

Miss Snow frowned. "Should she not be—"

"A fine idea," Brook agreed. "Then you shall not have to travel so far out of your way, Mrs. Lockhart."

"Do I not—" Chloe started.

"We shall see you for supper soon!" Mrs. Lockhart gave Chloe a wave and tugged Miss Snow away, practically pushing her into the carriage.

He pressed his lips together to suppress a grin. It seemed whatever he had done, he had done enough to assuage any of Mrs. Lockhart's suspicions. He would have to buy her something nice as a thank you for engineering some time alone with Chloe.

"Shall we?" he asked Chloe.

She glared at him for a few seconds then sighed. "Very well."

Following the road out of the village, it swiftly turned into a country road lined by hedgerows. The ruts were deeper here because the rain had few places to drain so when the roads were muddy, it was usually impassable. It meant watching their step so as not to trip over—something Chloe seemed to struggle to do. She stumbled twice and Brook had to jump into action to catch her.

The second time, she did not push away from him so fast. Her gaze caught on his and he could have sworn he heard her inhale sharply. Her fingers curled into his arm and he flexed his fingers against the small of her back. Her cheeks reddened and she straightened.

"I am not normally so clumsy."

"I beg to differ," he murmured with a smile.

"I am not. It just seems to be..." She scowled. "It seems to be when you are around," she admitted quietly.

He rather liked that admission.

"Your friends seem like pleasant girls."

"I think Joanna would object to the 'girls' part of that."

He grinned. "Yes, she is the epitome of a strong woman."

"The death of her husband did that to her, I think."

"It must have been quite a shock, to lose him so soon and at such a young age."

Chloe nodded. "I did not know her properly when it happened and she does not speak of it much, but how could it not affect her?"

"I was wondering when you became friends with them. I have never seen you with them before."

She peered at him. "I did not know you paid attention to my activities. I rather thought I was invisible to you."

"I had to keep an eye on the enemy, did I not?"

She pursed her lips. "You are correct, though. We came to know each other during the last Season. There is rather a drought of single women my age now. They are all married off."

"But not you."

"Yes, thank you for reminding me of that."

"I had rather thought you were not all that interested in marriage."

"I am not, I do think. At least, I have never met anyone to whom I would wish to be married. But it is rather a bore to be reminded of my unmarried status constantly and, of course, Mama would love for me to make a match before I am too old and horrible."

"It might be too late for that," he teased.

She swiped at his arm. "We cannot all be beautiful like you, Brook."

He dodged her hand. "You think I am beautiful?"

"You know full well you are attractive. Or at least some people think you are. I mean...that is..." She blew out a breath. "Cease teasing me."

"I am not alone in my attractiveness."

Turning her head to eye him, a red brow lifted and she laughed. "You cannot mean me."

"I do indeed."

"I am not being modest, I swear it, but I am hardly the sort to turn heads."

"You turn mine, Chloe."

Head tilted, she stared at him for a good few seconds more then looked away. They continued along the road in silence until they reached the fence leading into the fields. She stopped and waited.

"Farewell, Brook."

He ignored her comment and moved past her to unlatch the gate and swing it open, motioning for her to enter. She moved past him and he followed after her. Perhaps that kiss in the bookshop was making him too bold, but he could not help himself. The last thing he wanted to do at present was leave Chloe. If that meant traipsing along enemy ground, so be it.

She made a noise of annoyance and picked up her pace.

"Miss Larkin, are you trying to rid yourself of me?" He moved swiftly to keep up with her as they traipsed through ankle-length grass toward her land.

"Most certainly. If my father finds you here, he shall shoot you."

If her father found out he had kissed her, he would do worse than shoot him. He'd probably be hung, drawn, and quartered.

It had been a reckless move—perhaps one he regretted. They were hidden away and no one would find out about the kiss, but he suspected he would remember it for a long, long time. Her inexperience had been clear, especially when she had gone rigid in his arms but once he had helped her relax, by God, it was clear Chloe Larkin would become an expert on kissing very swiftly. Apparently there was something to be said for being a bookish wallflower. If other men realised these wallflowers could be so passionate, they would all be snapped up within moments.

They came upon the stile that indicated they would be stepping onto Larkin land. She stopped in front of it, turning around, and folded her arms across her chest.

"I never took you for a coward, Chloe."

"And I never took you for a fool." She ran her gaze up and down him. "Why are you doing this? You know we can meet at night, when it is safe."

He tugged off his hat and sank his fingers through his hair before placing it back. "Perhaps because I want to spend more time with you."

"But why?"

He had not had much time to think on it but his instincts never led him wrong. He had likely known it since he had first come upon her in the bookshop those weeks ago. "There is something between us, Chloe. I wish to see where it leads," he said frankly.

She blinked at him several times then twisted on her heel and clambered awkwardly over the stile, her skirts catching on the rough wood as she went. She stumbled down to the ground on the other side and continued walking away from him.

Following quickly, he made easy work of the fence and caught up to her. "Do I not even get a response?"

She stilled and faced him. "You should go home, Brook. It is too dangerous to be here."

"Did you hear what I said? I have feelings for you, Chloe. I think you have feelings for me too."

Her lips parted and he heard her draw in a shaky breath. She closed her eyes briefly and when she opened them, they were full of determination. "I had thought that perhaps all the gossip was incorrect. That you were a better man than people had said. I must have been wrong."

"Chloe—"

She began marching away from him again, cutting across the fields that would take her directly to the house. The very tips of the building could be seen and before long they would be viewable from the windows. Brook could not bring himself to care. He did not blame Chloe for not trusting him—after all he was the 'enemy' and his reputation was not one of a pure virgin. However, he had hoped she knew him well enough now to know he was not being insincere.

He caught up with her again, this time placing himself firmly in front of her. She put her hands to her hips and glared at him. "If you are spotted here..."

He shrugged. "Let them see me. I am not ashamed."

"I do not think you will be ashamed. But you might very well be dead."

Brook smirked. "I'm much faster than your father. He will struggle to shoot me."

She made a frustrated sound. "Go home, Brook. We can still plan whatever it is you wish to plan—just go home."

He shook his head. "Not until you stop ignoring what I just said."

She dropped her arms to her side. "Fine. If what you have said is indeed true—that you have feelings for me—it does not matter. I am a Larkin, and you are a Waverley. That is all there is to it."

"So your argument for us not being together is our families?"

She nodded.

"I think you are simply making excuses. I think perhaps you are scared, Chloe. For once in your life, you are unable to hide behind your books and in libraries."

"Scared? You do not scare me, Brook Waverley. But I have no wish to anger our families further."

"If you are not scared, you do an awfully good attempt at looking so." He took one of her hands. "Your hands are shaking."

"Because I am angry."

"What have I done to make you angry?"

She tried to tear her hand away from him but he kept hold of it. "Because I believe you find it amusing to toy with me."

"So it is not just our families' discord that is informing your decisions?"

Chloe tilted her head. "You know well of your reputation and I believe you take pride in it. Why should I believe you truly feel something for me? For all I know this could be part of some plan with your father to dishonor me and discredit my family."

"You truly believe I would do something as shameful as that?" He shook his head and released her hand. He did not blame her for her doubt, but he could not help but feel stung by that remark.

Folding her arms across her chest, she blew a strand of hair from her face. "I...I do not know."

He sensed her softening toward him and took the opportunity to close the gap between them. "I do know. I do know that you want to kiss me again. I do know that you enjoy my company. I do know that you have feelings for me and you are scared of them."

"I do not—"

He cut her off with a firm kiss upon her lips. She sank into him quickly, swiftly, even uttering a sound of gratification. Good God, he had been right. Chloe was a damned quick learner. He wrapped his arms about her and held her firm, feeling the soft flesh of her thighs pressed against his.

Kissing her deeply, he reveled in the taste of her until she was breathless. Then he broke away and she staggered a little. She stared at him for a few moments then made a show of straightening her skirts.

"This changes nothing, Brook," she said finally, her words so satisfyingly breathy.

It took all his willpower not to drag her into his arms again. He wasn't wrong—she was scared. But she would have to come to the realization on her own, he suspected. A woman like Chloe could not be forced into anything.

"I think we should arrange for our fathers to meet in town," he suggested.

Creases appeared between her brows and she blinked at him several times before nodding. "Yes, that could work."

"Excellent. I shall send word again soon once we have established how and where. I will talk with my father about taking a trip and you do the same with yours."

"O-of course."

"And, Chloe, there is no need to be scared."

"I am not—" She blew out a heavy breath. "I am going home, Brook. I suggest you do the same."

He watched her leave and waited until she vanished over the horizon, her speedy pace taking her out of his sight too quickly for his liking. He could not help but smile to himself, though. Her reaction told him all he needed to know—and it confirmed it all in his mind. He was falling for Miss Chloe Larkin and she was doing the same for him.

Chapter Thirteen

Steely gray clouds spread across the sky, an unwelcome blanket that hung heavy over the horizon. Chloe grimaced. This did not bode well for their plan. If it rained, her father might not wish to disembark from the carriage and might even return home. She glanced at her mother and father opposite her in the carriage, and her stomach bunched. All this plotting against her parents was making her uneasy even if she knew it was for the right reasons.

Because it was for the right reasons, was it not? It had nothing to do with wishing to see Brook and wondering if she might just get another kiss from him.

Or perhaps she really was that selfish and the reason she was continuing on with this was to see him again. No matter how foolish that made her. As much as she'd like to believe him, there was no way Mr. Brook Waverley had proper feelings for her. Even if he had some kind of stirrings, they would pass soon enough. There were many people who enjoyed her company and her knowledge born of books, but she was not silly enough to believe that her companionship would keep a man like him forever entertained.

She blew out a breath and twined her fingers together, focusing her attention on the lace trim around her gloves. The kiss—and the talk of his feelings—was done. She needed to move on and focus on what they were doing here.

Beside her, Freddie fidgeted, huffing because he felt Chloe took up all the space on the seat. She hoped things went well, for her brother's sake as much as her. Freddie could do without witnessing an argument between the two men.

She stole another glance at her father. He looked tired today, with dark circles around his eyes. When she had suggested they might all travel into town together and partake in tea, her father had seemed keen on the idea.

If he was curious as to her sudden need for his company, she did not know, but since their failed walk, he had been keen to make it up to her. If anything, that made her feel worse about the deception. However, this needed to be done. He was likely tired because he had been up early and angry over the border. Yet again, the fence was back over their side and her father had been barking orders for it to be moved immediately. It was no wonder he was not doing well with this matter causing him so much stress.

Tightness gathered in her throat when they reached the fountain in the middle of the town. The fountain was where she had suggested she and Brook meet. The carriages could circle around, drop off their passengers and return to collect them later. It was the ideal place for them to all meet oh so accidentally.

Her heartbeat increased when she recognized the Waverleys' carriage departing the circular road around the fountain. Brook spotted her looking out of the carriage window and gave her the briefest nod before turning his attention back to his father. This was it then. They were finally going to get their fathers if not in the same room, then in the same town. She only hoped the public setting would prevent them from doing anything too drastic to one another.

The carriage came to a halt, rocking on its suspension. Chloe offered her father a shaky smile as he handed her down. All this deception was beginning to drive her mad. That would at least explain why she was letting herself get involved with a man like Brook. It might even account for why she had been so keen to kiss him.

Yes, she rather liked the sound of that. It was just madness that was doing this to her. As soon as they repaired their fathers' relationships, the better, and then she could put an end to this madness.

She waited for her father to spot George Waverley. She dare not look directly at them but she could see Brook conversing with his father and no doubt trying to delay his departure from the area. Chloe's mother fussed with her skirts and her hat, buying them time for both men to see one another, even though her mother had little idea she was doing such a thing. If her mama knew what was going on, Chloe would be in for a reprimand indeed. As tired as they both were of the arguments, her mother would inevitably take her father's side and wanted a peaceful life, which usually meant indulging her husband's argument with the Waverleys.

"What the bloody hell is he doing here?"

Chloe snapped her head around, her stomach curdling with dread. Her father's attention was fixed on George Waverley and she could see the fury building in his gaze. He balled his fists at his sides, and redness tinged his cheeks. Chloe pressed a hand to her chest. Oh Lord, what a mistake this had been. How naive they were to imagine that either of their fathers might be able to have a civilized conversation simply because they were on display. After all, everyone knew of the argument between the two families. It was public knowledge and therefore they had nothing to hide.

Brook's father finally glanced their way and Chloe held her breath. She saw the same anger quickly take over his expression, and she shared a look with Brook. He perhaps had not quite come to the realization that she had—that this was all a massive mistake—but she saw the apprehension in his expression. Mr. Waverley marched over to them, his gait slightly lopsided, revealing the toll his recent heart attack had taken. Her own father was no quicker but both men still closed the gap between them with enough speed that Chloe and Brook had to hurry to catch up with them.

"You moved the damn fence again," her father said, thrusting a finger Mr. Waverley's way.

"Of course I did. I was taking back my land. As I am well within my rights to do," Mr. Waverley bellowed.

"It is not your damned land, when will you get that through your thick skull, George?"

"Just about the same time when you stop being a callous bastard," Mr. Waverley spat.

Her father snorted. "Callous bastard? You're a fine one to talk."

"I'm not the one responsible for the death of an innocent woman." George Waverley took a step closer.

Chloe sent a desperate look Brook's way. Somehow, they needed to get their fathers to calm down but she could not fathom how. Brook stepped in between the two men, his hands held, palm out, to halt both of them. "I do not think we need to fight, gentlemen. This is not the time nor the place."

"Fight?" Mr. Waverley said. "I'll fight him anytime. Anytime, anywhere."

"Gladly!" Her father straightened his shoulders. "I'll fight you right here, Waverley. And I'll take great pleasure in seeing you beaten."

Brook shook his head. "No one needs to be beaten here today. Especially not in front of your wife and children, Mr. Larkin." Brook sent a pointed look Chloe and her mother's way.

Her mother clung to her arm. "If they fight, both men will end up dead. Neither of them have the strength."

"Father is strong enough to best him," Freddie muttered.

Chloe nodded. She and Brook had underestimated their fathers' desire for blood. She might have expected some cross words, but she certainly did not expect them to leap to the idea of fighting immediately.

"Don't you tell me what to do in front of my children," snapped her father. Turning his attention on to Brook.

"Don't you tell my son what to do." Mr. Waverley squared his shoulders and faced her father head on.

"Everyone is looking, Chloe," her brother said, tucking himself behind their mother as his freckled cheeks reddened.

A crowd had begun to gather around them. Chloe unhooked her mother's arms from hers, patting the back of her hand. If she did not do something soon, she suspected it really would come to fisticuffs. She stepped up to the two men as they raised their fists. Brook had already inserted himself fully in between them, however, they continued to shout at each other as though he was not even there.

"Stop!" Chloe stamped down a foot and put a hand on her father's chest, then to Mr. Waverley's.

Both men froze. She turned her attention to her father first, ensuring that he made eye contact with her. "Stop," she said more softly this time. "This is not how a gentleman behaves." She turned to face Mr. Waverley. "I do not care how much you two hate each other, this is not the way to act in public. I am ashamed of both of you. What an example you are setting to your children."

"Look, Freddie is watching your every move. Do you wish him to behave the same when he grows up? You wish for him to be fighting in public? Airing all of his private business?" she demanded of her father.

He gave a grunt.

Brook gave her a brief but grateful look. This had not gone how either of them had planned and Chloe was beginning to wonder why they ever thought it would be any different. Decades of bad blood between the family was not going to be ended by one quick meeting. If they were to ever fix this—good Lord, she could not fathom how—it would take a lot more than a chance meeting.

"She's right, Father," Brook agreed. "You are both making a scene."

"I did not make a scene. He started it." His father puffed out his chest.

"Why you—" Chloe's father began.

"Father!" Chloe snapped. "That is enough." She forcibly took her father's arm and began to walk away. She thought he might fight her on it, but he relented, allowing her to take him back to the carriage. It did not prevent him from shooting daggers at George Waverley, however.

She could hear Mr. Waverley muttering angry words under his breath. She corralled her father back into the carriage, and her mother swiftly settled next to him. Freddie leaned his head far out of the coach to eye Brook and his father.

"Marcus, you really shouldn't have," her mother said softly, tugging Freddie back into the carriage by his jacket.

Freddie simply looked amused by it all. "I think you should have punched him, Father."

"Freddie!" Mama scolded.

"If he had punched him," Chloe told her little brother, "they might well have ended up in jail. You wish our father to be dead?"

"I could have bested him," her father grumbled. "He's weak after a heart attack. He is a weak old man."

"And you are no sprightly lad," her mother said with a little more bite than Chloe might have expected.

Her father snapped his mouth shut after shooting his wife a surprised look. Settling back in the carriage, he tugged his hat over his face and closed his eyes, pretending to sleep. At least he was no longer spouting threats of duels and beating up Mr. Waverley.

Chloe watched Brook and his father still standing by the fountain as the carriage rolled away. He shot her the briefest, regretful look before his father could spot him. They would have to meet again, and soon if they were going to fix what had happened. She suspected their meddling may have made things even worse. Especially now that her little brother had seen what had gone on and seemed to think it all highly amusing.

Her mother tapped Chloe's hand, giving her knuckles a little rub. "Do not be upset, Chloe. I have witnessed too many of these arguments and they all turn out the same. Both men will go off, fight about the border a little longer, and hopefully never see each other again."

Chloe could not decide if she was more upset over the events of today or whether she had been so foolish to think that she could fix so much anger within one day. It seemed to her that the fates were completely against the families ever coming to an agreement. And that had to mean, there was no chance there could ever be anything between her and Brook. Even if she had, for one silly moment, believed his words yesterday.

Chapter Fourteen

"You must take me for a fool, boy," Brook's father said, thrusting a finger in his direction over the dinner table.

"I am not at all certain what you mean," Brook said nonchalantly.

His mother arched an eyebrow at them both but remained quiet, concentrating on her dinner. She had already heard all about the argument today but had wisely remained quiet on the matter. Though Brook was tempted to scold his father for his behavior, it would do no good.

He and Chloe had severely underestimated the anger both of their fathers held. He grimaced. He was sorry for getting Chloe involved in the matter now. She had looked on the verge of tears by the time they left, though she had done an outstanding job of standing up to their fathers.

"This outing today. I had wondered why you might want to visit town with your father. Now I know why. This is some misguided notion of getting me to talk to Marcus."

Brook frowned and wondered whether he should try to lie. He should have known his father would see through the invite. If they were to spend time together, they were more likely to go hunting than take a drink in town.

"I had heard you spent time with that Larkin girl at the ball. Whatever hold she has over you, you would be wise to let it go."

Brook glanced at his mother who simply shrugged. "A mere dance, Father. I have danced with many women. It means nothing." The words felt like a bitter lie on his tongue.

His father jabbed a fork in his direction. "Stay away from her," he warned. "All Larkins are the same. She will seduce you and use you, mark my words."

Brook could not help but smile at the idea of Chloe using him. He would not mind the seduction, however, she was hardly the sort to do such a thing. If his father only knew Chloe, he was certain he would like her very much. God knew, Brook liked her an immense amount. So much so that he was thinking there might be another way to rectify the situation between the families.

"Son, I mean it."

Brook did not bother to argue. There was no point when his father was in such a mood. If anything, this whole matter simply made him more determined to fix things between the families, especially seeing how upset Chloe was.

His mother cleverly managed to direct the conversation away from anything to do with today so that the rest of the evening was peaceful, though, his father tried to divert the conversation back to those 'damned Larkins' when he could.

Brook waited until both of his parents had retired to bed before heading out under the cover of darkness. In the distance, an owl hooted and a half-moon revealed itself behind the clouds in intermittent moments. A fresh breeze rustled the few trees around the house, but it was not cold.

They had not discussed another meeting and he doubted Chloe had found time to leave him a message, but this could not wait. He needed to speak with her urgently. He marched into the stables, managing not to disturb the groomsmen who slept in the accommodations above the small stables and saddled his horse.

Riding partway to her house, he left his horse tethered on the outskirts of the gardens to avoid detection by any servants still awake. "Be a good girl," he told her, giving her a pat.

Chloe's house was a square Tudor building. Generous in size with presumably an open courtyard in the center and the front door framed by a large stone entrance way. The gardens still maintained the organized look the Tudors favored, with straight lines of bushes segmenting the flowerbeds.

Lamplight shone in several of the windows on the upper story but the rest of the house was dark. He knew which bedroom Chloe's was because she had mentioned views over the gardens. At least he hoped he was right or else he could cause even more trouble.

He launched a small stone at the window, satisfied when it made a loud ping noise. He waited a few moments and tried again. She could be asleep, he supposed, but he had his doubts after today's events. He tried a third time and saw the curtains part and Chloe press her face against the glass. He gave her a wave and she eased open the window. "What are you doing here?" she hissed. "It is too dangerous. Go away." She fluttered a hand out of the window, shooing him away.

"I'm not going anywhere until you come down here," he told her.

She hesitated, perhaps deciding whether she could persuade him to leave but apparently she realised she did not have a hope in hell of sending him away. She closed the window and he waited, tapping his foot until the sound of padded footsteps and a shadowy outline made him smile.

"You should not be here," she whispered.

He took her hand, ignoring her words, and began to lead her away from the house.

"Wait, where are we going? What are we doing?" She tugged on his hand.

"You said I should not be here."

"Yes, *you*. I should be here. In fact, I should be in bed."

"We need to talk about today." He glanced back at her, noting that she was still in her nightwear, which was wrapped in an awkwardly tied gown. Even though the night was dark, the white fabric revealed her outline like a ghost haunting the night. It made his palms itch when he considered that there was probably very little between her skin and the night air. But, for now, he needed to keep his thoughts away from such matters. They would not help his cause at all.

"Brook, where are we going?" she pressed.

"Somewhere we can talk."

She made a sound of annoyance but did not ask him any more questions and allowed him to tug her along until they reached his horse. "Get on," he ordered.

He suspected she rolled her eyes at him but he missed it. Even so, she climbed up on the horse with his help, settling at the front of the pommel and allowing him to get on behind her. He took the reins, enveloping her and settling her across his lap. With her soft bottom nestled into his lap, every part of him was on fire. He gritted his teeth and tried to ignore the subtle scent of flowers that came from her hair. Now was not the time to be thinking of all the devilish things he would like to do to her.

He rode at a gentler pace toward the spot by the river that was past either of their lands. An ancient stone bridge across the river and he brought his horse to a halt just by it. Dismounting, he handed Chloe down, and allowed himself just a few more moments of touching her until he released her to light the two lanterns that were set on poles either side of the bridge. They were rarely lit these days as the bridge was ill-used, but it would be a lot easier to talk to her with a little light.

"You know, we could have waited and spoken at the border." She folded her arms and gave a little shudder.

Brook grimaced and removed his jacket, throwing it around her shoulders even as she made a sound of protest. She quickly huddled into the fabric, and Brook smiled.

"What is it?"

"I was just thinking how fine you look in my jacket."

She frowned then yawned, covering her mouth with one hand. "What are we doing out here, Brook?"

He swallowed hard. There was a small chance he had not thought this moment through properly, however, he was never one to dawdle. He needed to act now.

"We need to fix this, Chloe." He took her hand to lead her to the middle of the bridge and leaned over to look into the water.

She followed suit. "It was rather a disaster. I am not certain how we can fix this, however."

"I have an idea."

"Oh?"

He twisted to face her, and took one of her hands, urging her to meet his gaze. His hand trembled a little and his heart picked up its pace. He never imagined he would get to this point in his life, especially with a Larkin of all people. Especially Chloe Larkin. She was smart, and bookish, and a wallflower, and far more opinionated than anyone he had ever met. She was also funny and kind and dutiful. She was many, many things, and he suspected there was still more for him to find out.

"Brook?" She frowned at him. "What is wrong? If it is about today, we shall do our best to figure something else out. I know how much you want to repair the relationship between our families."

"I do indeed."

"We shall think of something. I will still help, I promise."

He allowed himself a smile. He doubted anything other than what he had planned would resolve the matter. Perhaps even this would not work. But he had to try.

"I have an idea. In fact, I think it might be the best idea I have ever had."

She chuckled. "Better than our fathers nearly having a fight in the middle of town?"

"Yes, perhaps that was not the finest of ideas. I think we underestimated quite how angry and willing to fight our fathers are. However, they will not be able to fight over this."

"Fight over what?"

He kept her hand in his, and he wasn't certain if she'd even noticed. It was ridiculous to feel so nervous about such a matter. How many brave and bold things had he done and never felt any nerves whatsoever.

"Well, it is quite obvious really."

She made an exasperated noise. "What is?"

"We marry, of course."

She blinked at him several times, slowly. "Marry?" she echoed.

Brook nodded. "It makes perfect sense."

"Perfect sense?"

He chuckled. "Have I broken you?"

She tilted her head back and peered at him. "You speak of the idea so matter-of-factly."

"If we marry, our parents will have no choice but to reconcile. Then, when I inherit my father's estate, we can solve the boundary issue with your brother."

"I–I know you are keen to fix this problem, Brook, but marriage seems a little extreme. I am certain there are other ways."

He frowned. "You have no desire to marry me?"

She hesitated, just long enough for him to see something in her expression that gave him hope. He wasn't certain what he had expected or that he had rather expected she would be keen on the idea.

"I had never really considered marrying but I certainly never considered partaking in one as an act of duty."

"But, Chloe, why should we not marry? You have no other plans to marry, do you?"

Chloe tugged her hand away from his, her gaze narrowing. "If you are asking as to whether I have other offers, no I do not, as you are fully aware. That does not mean I'm going to leap at the first offer that comes my way. If I were ever to marry, I had rather hoped it might be for love, and not duty."

Brook cursed under his breath. What a royal mess he had made of this. Somehow he had thought appealing to Chloe's practical sense of nature might be more useful than appealing to her emotions.

"I did not picture marrying anytime soon either. But that was before I met you, Chlo."

"What do you mean?"

"If we were to marry, I'm certain it would fix the problems between our families. However, I should also like to marry you out of love."

There, he had said it. The words are out there, as they probably should have been in the first place. It was the one and only time he had ever asked a woman to marry him and, he had to admit, he should have planned it better.

"Love?" she repeated.

He gave a crooked grin. "Indeed."

"You love me?"

He nodded.

"But that's impossible," she spluttered.

"No, it is entirely possible."

She shook her head vigorously. "You are Mr. Brook Waverley, the infamous rake. You could have any woman you wanted."

"The woman I want is standing right in front of me. Is it so hard to believe that I might be telling the truth?"

She folded her arms across her chest. "Well...yes, it is. I have known for a very long time I am not the sort of woman who captures a man's attention, and I made my peace with it. I would certainly never have expected an offer from a man like you." She sighed. "I know how keen you are to settle this matter, and how worried you are for your father. I do not believe you make such an offer with any malice, but I do believe you are not thinking straight."

Brook took her hand again. "Believe me, Chloe, I have never been so straight thinking in my life."

"I cannot marry you, Brook. How can I? My father would never forgive me and it would not be long before you would resent giving up your lifestyle." Her mouth opened a little. "Unless, of course, you plan to be one of these men who leave their wife at home while they go out and indulge whatever needs they have." She gave a little shudder. "I would rather remain a spinster than have one of those marriages."

"I had hoped you might know me better than that."

Her gaze searched his and she blew out a breath. "I cannot marry you."

"Just think on the matter. I think, given time, you will realize that you can trust me. You might also realize that you love me too." He grinned at her shocked face. "You do not have to give me an answer now," he added before giving her a swift kiss on the lips.

"But I have given you my answer."

"Take your time." He gave her another kiss. "I am more than willing to wait."

Her exasperated expression amused him and he could not bring himself to feel downhearted about the matter. She just needed a little persuading. They were a good match, and she would realize that soon enough. Nor did he blame her for being cautious—after all he was no saint. The more time they spent together, however, the more she would realize that he was sincere about this. If he had to wait an eternity for Chloe, he would.

He loved Chloe Larkin, he knew that with every fiber of his being.

Chapter Fifteen

"I am sorry to say, Chloe, the news of your father getting into a fight has spread far and wide," Joanna said, taking a sip of tea.

Chloe grimaced and sat on the sofa next to Augusta. She did not even bother reaching for her cup of tea, nor any of the delicious treats that had been prepared for them. It was not just her father's near fight that made her stomach turn, however.

No, she was very certain it was almost all Brook.

How could he propose to her like that? How could he just fling the question at her, as though it were not some great, life-changing matter? How could he declare he loved her?

The funny thing was, he had done it in such a Brook-like manner. She was beginning to understand that he always barreled through life without really stopping and worrying about the consequences of his actions. She rather liked his bravery most of the time, however, being told that one should marry out of duty was not what she wanted.

And then he had declared he loved her...

"Was it so very terrible?" Augusta asked.

Chloe shook her head. "I did fear they were going to fight physically but it is not that..." She glanced around the parlor room, flitting her gaze from the teal green wall coverings to the elegant wood fireplace and then finally back to Augusta.

Joanna narrowed her gaze at her. "It is about Brook, is it not?"

Reaching for the cup of tea, Chloe focused her attention on the tawny liquid inside for want of something else to stay. Her friends knew of her growing friendship with Brook—and Joanna had even encouraged it—but would they think her foolish for believing him, even if just for a moment? The gilded clock on the mantel ticked by the seconds, and she could feel her friends' gazes upon her.

Finally, she lowered the cup, untouched, and lifted her head. "He asked me to marry him," she said softly.

"Marry?" Augusta spluttered and dropped her tea swiftly onto the coffee table as she choked on the sip she had been taking. Joanna stood and gave her a little tap on the back until she recovered while Chloe fished out a handkerchief and handed it over. Augusta dabbed her lips and gave an apologetic smile. "Forgive me. It is just that everyone knows Mr. Brook Waverley is not in the market for marriage."

"Well, he was not until he got to know Chloe." Joanna grinned.

Augusta lifted a hand. "I do not mean to disparage you, Chloe. You know I love you dearly and think any man would be lucky to have you. Which is why it is hard to imagine you with such a rake of a man."

Chloe nodded. "You are not wrong. At least, I cannot deny that I felt the same. *Still* feel the same. Or..." She paused and frowned, dropping her face into her hands. "I do not know what I feel," she said against her palms.

Joanna gave her a gentle rub on the back, and Chloe lifted her head. She glanced sideways at her friend who had a somewhat knowing smile upon her face.

"Augusta is not wrong. He is a rake. We all know of his reputation."

"Men change," Augusta said, "and if anyone could change a man, it would be you, Chloe."

"What exactly were his reasons for asking?" Joanna leaned forward. "He believes your match could repair the rift between the families?"

Chloe should not be surprised by Joanna's assumption. It was, of course, what she had assumed first.

"He did suggest that such a thing would help our families." Chloe sat back and nibbled on the end of a thumb.

"Well, I know you would never get married simply out of duty. So what is the problem?" Joanna's lips curved ever so slightly.

Blast, even Joanna knew the reason for the conflict. Brook declared that she loved him, but how could she? She had counselled herself against any feelings toward him at every turn while they had been together. After all, he was charming and handsome and well used to getting his way with women. It would be ridiculous to fall for such a man.

She chewed on the end of her thumb for a few moments more. "I suppose...I suppose my concern is that I might...feel something for him."

"But does he feel something for you?" Augusta asked. "You would not wish to be married to a man who does not love you."

"He more than feels something for me." Chloe opened her palms. "He said that he loves me."

Augusta clapped her hands together. "Oh, how wonderful. Well, then what is the problem?"

"Chloe does not know how she feels," Joanna said.

Chloe pursed her lips. "Joanna is not wrong. Can I really take him at his word? What if he thought he needed to say that to sway me into marriage simply for the sakes of our fathers? After all, Mr. Waverley had a heart attack. If Brook wishes to save him strain, I would understand him wanting to do anything to help his father."

Joanna tatted. "Firstly, do you really believe he is capable of such a thing?" She held up a hand. "I am aware of his reputation—have read all of the gossip columns myself—and even warned you of his reputation before. However, you have good instincts, Chloe. If you like the man, and even have feelings for him, I would trust your instincts. And, secondly, though the marriage might heal the rift between your families in future, do you really believe both fathers will be happy about the match? I highly doubt they would welcome it."

"If that is the case," Augusta interjected, "then it would be against his best interests to ask to marry you."

Chloe inhaled deeply. That was true too. If she told her father she was getting engaged to Brook, goodness knows what he would do. No matter which way she looked at it, it seemed impossible. She could trust Brook and trust her own feelings and marry him and maybe leave herself open to injury as well as disappointing her father, or she could continue to deny him...and deny herself. Though it might not fix everything between their families, at least her father would not be angry with her.

"This seems impossible." Chloe dropped her head to her hands once more.

"It is a difficult decision indeed," Augusta agreed.

"I think you need to be more certain of your feelings," Joanna suggested. "If you were, you would not feel so conflicted."

Chloe lifted her head to her friend.

"Do not forget," Joanna said, "you had resigned yourself to a life of being a spinster wallflower. Now it is all changed overnight. Be kind to yourself, Chloe. This is not the sort of decision you should make lightly."

"Yes, you are right." Chloe smiled gratefully. "Thank goodness I have you two fellow wallflowers or else I would be entirely lost."

"Augusta and I have to live vicariously through someone!" Joanna chuckled.

"You know you can always come to us." Augusta leaned in and gave Chloe a little squeeze around the waist.

A light tap on the door was followed by Chloe's lady's maid entering. "Forgive me, miss, but your father wants a word with you." Some sort of warning flittered across Mary's expression. Dread pooled in her stomach. Whatever this was, it could not be good.

Joanna rose. "We shall leave you but should you wish to...um... go somewhere where a certain other person might be, do not be shy. I am always happy to play escort."

Chloe smiled gratefully and embraced both of her friends. She rather wished they would stay by her side for the next several weeks until she had handled this Brook situation and her father. It was all becoming a bit much to face on one's own.

After she waved her friends off, she made her way to her father's study, moving slowly past the portraits of ancestors that lined the corridor. Pressing a hand to her stomach, Chloe straightened the sleeves of her gown and tapped her knuckles lightly on the study door. Whatever her father wanted, it was likely not to be a good thing. The last time she had been summoned to the study like so she had been fourteen and had been in trouble for teasing her younger brother too much. What had she done now, she did not know, but she was not looking forward to this.

"Come in," came her father's voice, gruff and abrupt.

She twisted the doorknob, the clicking sound seeming like the loudest noise in the world. She closed the door behind her, wincing at the creak of hinges, before facing her father. This was silly, and she was not a child anymore. But he was still her father and the last thing she ever wanted to do was disappoint him. What exactly had she done?

She waited a few moments while he finished off a letter, the quill scratching across the paper with quick efficiency. The room was dark, with the curtains semi-drawn. He wrote by lamplight and the scent of the lit wick infused the air. He seemed to take a long time to finish the letter then blotted it slowly as though reveling in her discomfort. She stared at her shoes, eyeing the peach bows and tracing each loop in her mind.

Finally, he looked up at her. Looping his hands together on top of the table, he ran his gaze up and down her. "Do I not give you many freedoms?"

"Yes, Papa." Chloe frowned.

"Would you not say that you have many more freedoms than other women of your age?"

She nodded, biting down on her bottom lip. Her stomach began to hurt. No wonder she'd suffered misgivings. She had a horrible feeling she knew where this was going.

"I have never pressured you into marriage. Nor have I forced you to partake in activities that you do not enjoy. I let you spend time with your friends and have that Mrs. Lockhart to escort you around." His jaw tightened and his cheeks reddened.

Gone was the frail, tired old man, she had feared was ageing too rapidly. The tightness in her stomach spread up to her chest, making her heart beat faster.

"Do I not give you all of these things?"

She nodded again.

"Do I not?" he demanded.

"Yes, Papa," she said rapidly.

"Then why is it, that I hear of you sneaking out at night, to meet with the most scandalous of men?" he bit out tersely.

Chloe inhaled sharply. She should have known. Maybe she did. But she did not care. How much longer did she really expect to keep slipping out of the house and not be caught? Goodness knows who it was who had spotted her—maybe it was even her father who could not sleep or one of the servants. It did not matter, though, did it? The only thing that mattered now was that her father knew, and she was in a world of trouble.

"Papa..." she started, uncertain of what she could possibly say to defend herself. She briefly considered trying to lie or claim that someone was mistaken, that she was simply walking because she could not sleep, but she suspected that would just make the situation worse.

He thrust a finger at her. "Do not try to defend yourself, Chloe. I had expected better of you. I thought you were a clever girl but I was wrong. Not only do you risk ruin, you risk it with a man of such ill repute that you would see your name and the family's name splashed across the papers. You have been inconsiderate indeed."

Chloe stared at the painting behind her father's head. She had always hated it—some gruesome medieval battle where horses and soldiers were wounded upon the floor, spears protruding out of their bodies. She shuddered. Never before had the painting seemed so ominous.

What could she even say? Her father was not lying. Her reasons for meeting Brook might have been somewhat unselfish but after a while...well, she could not deny that the meetings were for herself. Brook was right. She had fallen for him.

"It seems to me that you cannot be trusted and therefore I must put your future in my hands."

She snapped her head up. "What do you mean?"

"I mean, I shall make a marriage for you. I had thought you had little interest in the opposite sex but apparently I was wrong. Therefore, I think it prudent to find you a match as quickly as possible."

"No, Papa, please—"

"It is practically settled, Chloe. I have a man in mind. He is of good means and character. I have no doubt you shall be a good match."

Panic burst in her chest, fluttering like the wings of a trapped bird. She had been lucky that her parents had never pressured her into marriage. They knew that Freddie would eventually inherit and ensure she was looked after in later life. Her mother was the romantic sort and always hoped Chloe might find love. Thus, she had been left to her own devices. Until now.

She glanced at the contorted faces of the dying men in the painting, feeling rather like she had been stabbed in the chest by a spear too. "I do not want a good match." She moved closer to the desk. "Please, Papa. I cannot marry a stranger."

"He is not a stranger, at least not to me. Mr. James Lawrence. I think you shall find he is quite suitable."

Chloe pursed her lips. "Mr. Lawrence? Is he not closer to your age than mine?"

"Yes, and I think you will find you are quite suited. He has a love of books and reading as do you. He also lives a quiet and scandal-free lifestyle. I know he is in the market for a wife since his previous one passed so I think the match is quite suitable."

She shook her head slowly and the world began to blur. Everything became too loud—from the bird tweeting outside to the slight fizz of the lamp wick burning. She would not have been surprised if the world crumbled away beneath her feet.

She had expected him to be angry should he ever find out, but there was no chance she could have anticipated this.

"Is this because I was spending time with a man, or is it because he is the son of your enemy?"

Her father's expression darkened. "It is both," he snapped. "It is because you clearly do not put the family's interests first."

"Of course I do! I've always put the family's interests first. In fact, almost everything I do—"

"I will not hear anything more of it. And I'd better not hear of you leaving this house again without your mother."

"So you would keep me prisoner until this Mr. Lawrence comes to marry me? Whether I want it or not?"

"What you want is irrelevant, Chloe. You have proven that. You cannot be trusted to make your own choices."

"You are no better than Mr. Waverley," she snapped.

"Whatever do you mean by that?"

"I know of your marriage. Of how you saved that woman. Now you wish to do what Mr. Waverley wanted to do to that lady? You two are as bad as each other." Heat flowed through her fingertips, making her palms hot and clammy. No matter his flaws, she knew her father loved her, but he was not thinking sensibly right now. He never had when it came to the Waverleys. She could not believe he would go as far as to arrange a match for her with a stranger.

He narrowed his gaze at her. "How do you know about that?"

"I know more than you realize." Chloe folded her arms across her chest.

"It does not matter. None of this matters. You should do as I tell you for a change or there shall be consequences."

"I hardly think these consequences are fair." Tears burned at the corners of her eyes and her throat ached.

"Life is not fair." Her father turned his attention back to his letters. "You are dismissed, Chloe. I suggest you go and apologize to your mother too. She is quite upset that you would risk your reputation like this."

Chloe's chin wobbled. How could he do this to her? She understood his anger but to do such a thing...? She had clearly underestimated her father's hatred of the Waverleys. Her father kept his head bent low, and she fought the tears for a few moments, words boiling in her mind. But she suspected none of them would work.

Escaping the study, she dashed upstairs to her room, flinging herself on her bed. She buried her face into the pillow and willed the tears away. She would not cry like some child or a scorned woman. However, she would not marry Mr. Lawrence. Especially not now.

If anything, her father's declaration had done the opposite of what he had intended. She knew now. She loved Mr. Brook Waverley.

Chapter Sixteen

Brook eyed his father. Though it was a pleasant day, he had a blanket around his shoulders as he sat in the garden. Brook grimaced. Some days his father seemed as strong as ever but other days his age truly showed. Today did not seem the right time to tell him about Chloe or his plans to court her. But, damn it, he would have to tell them eventually.

Straightening his shoulders, he strode toward his father only to spot his mother in the formal gardens, waving at him. "Brook," she called.

Brook sighed. He did not much mind having to put off this conversation with his father but really, he wished to get it over and done with. The sooner he did, the sooner he could pursue Chloe formally. Then, all he had to do was persuade Chloe his intentions were good.

He followed the path around the house and walked toward his mother, slowing his pace when he realised why she wanted him. His boots felt suddenly leaden when he spied the woman sitting on a bench.

Judith Somerset.

A previous, much mistaken conquest of his. Not that his mother knew that. The young widow was attractive and confident, but she also had little to say for herself and had been keen on dominating Brook for a time. He had very quickly broken things off once he realised quite what she was truly like. However, she and his mother had become companions of a sort since then. Brook always suspected she had done it deliberately, to get close to him. As yet he had managed to avoid her.

He kept his expression neutral as he approached his mother and Judith. He could feel Judith's gaze upon him and an excessive perfume drifted toward him. "Did you need me, Mother?"

"I thought you might like to show Mrs. Somerset the new rock garden."

"Surely you can show her, Mother. Unfortunately I am—"

"What a wonderful idea." Judith leapt to her feet, and forcibly pressed her arm through his.

Brook grimaced. Apparently the time apart had not changed her nature at all. And for some reason, his mother seemed to be encouraging the behavior. She glanced at him with a satisfied look, and gave a small nod, as if to give her approval of the match. It seemed while he had not been paying attention, Judith had done quite a significant amount of work on his mother.

He bit back a sigh and motioned toward the rock garden. "This way." His mother might seem mild for the most part, but she had a fiercer temper than his father when she wanted to. Besides which, a moment alone with Judith would allow him to put to rest any ideas she might have. Particularly, if his mother had been encouraging her.

"It is so good to see you again, Brook. I seem to miss you every time I'm in London."

"Oh, really?" he said vaguely. There had been a few places where he deliberately avoided her. He did not much like having to run away from a woman, but Judith was the most determined sort and, for the most part, unlikely to listen to reason. He could only hope that had changed.

He adopted a brisk pace, forcing Judith to shuffle along next to him. "And, here we are," he announced. "The rock garden."

The garden was recently installed under the supervision of his mother. Exotic plants that did not enjoy the normal, damp ground of England, had been specially sourced and planted in the buildup of rocks that had been carefully arranged around a winding path. At the end of the path, a shallow pond was dotted with waterlilies. Even if Brook could tell Judith much about the plants, he had no desire to. The sooner this was over the better.

"Well, this is lovely," Judith said. "I can see why your mother is so proud of it."

"Indeed," he said tightly.

She eased her arm out of his and twisted to face him, forcing him to come to a stop halfway along the path. "As you might have noticed, your mother and I have become quite good friends. She is an excellent woman and I admire her greatly."

Brook gave a grunt. He could not argue with that.

"And," she twirled a raven curl around one of her fingers, "I do think she rather likes me. In fact, I would go as far as to say she is immensely fond of me." She gave a smile that reminded him of a cat just prior to him catching a mouse.

He had no intention of being caught.

"Well, now that you have seen the rock garden, why do you not head back inside? I am certain my mother is missing you if she is so fond of you as you just stated."

She perfected a pout. Once upon a time, he'd found Judith extremely attractive. With glossy raven hair, an excellent sense of fashion, and a figure she used to her advantage, it was hard to ignore her when she'd shown interest in him several years ago.

He could curse himself for rushing headlong into bed with her without knowing what she was like. She was vacuous, vain, and cared little for other's feelings. He could not say all of his lovers had been intellects, but he enjoyed conversation as much as a tumble and liked both from his partners.

"You have not shown it all to me." She pushed a curl from her face then let her fingers linger on her face and down to her décolletage.

Brook ignored the movement and debated his options. He could abandon her here but as much as he disliked her, it went against everything that had been ingrained in him. Cursing his upbringing, he motioned down the path.

"Let us continue then."

Judith smiledm and he caught the glint of satisfaction in her eyes. Maybe he could use this time to ensure she understood he had no interest in her whatsoever.

Though, he had tried to make it clear many times before so he was not certain why he thought this might finally work.

"I am surprised you are in Hampshire, Brook. I had thought you might still be in London. I was there last week and was disappointed not to see you."

"Unfortunately, Mrs. Somerset," he said with the emphasis on her name, "my father was ill. You might have heard."

"Oh yes, what a terrible thing to happen." She laid a hand on his arm. "I wish I could have been here to comfort you."

Her insincere tone combined with her touch sent a shiver down his spine. He doubted she cared one jot as to his father's health.

"And here is the pond," he announced, gesturing to the lily-scattered patch of water. Gray rocks, their edges smooth, surrounded it and the occasional ripple announced the presence of fish beneath the surface. It was a peaceful part of the garden and Judith did not fit in with the surroundings one bit here.

"Hmmm." She strolled around the edge of the pond, glancing back at him as she tugged off one of her gloves with her teeth. "You know, this is a quiet spot. Very private." She circled back around until standing in front of him once more. "I have missed you, Brook." She trailed her bare hand over his chest.

Brook took a step back.

"Do not tell me you have not missed me."

"I am sorry if I have not made it clear previous, Mrs. Somerset, but I have no intention of rekindling our...relationship."

"But your mother loves me! Do you not see how perfect it would be? We could marry and she would have a daughter she adores!"

"My mother loves you, but I do not," he said bluntly.

Judith released a laugh that made him wince. "Does that matter?" She shifted closer. "We are a perfect match, Brook. I am tired of being alone and we look so wonderful together."

He lifted a brow.

"And you cannot deny that we match wonderfully in bed too."

"Judith, I am not interested in marrying you and none of those are good enough reasons."

She made a dismissive noise. "Plenty of people marry for fewer reasons than that. You will not find another woman like me, I promise you that much."

He fought hard not to slap a palm to his forehead. She was nothing if not determined. He had no desire to bring Chloe into the matter, but she was one hundred times the woman Judith was.

"I think we had better head back. My mother shall be missing your company."

Her lips pursed. "You do not wish to take advantage of the time alone?"

"No, Judith, I do not. And I never will."

She narrowed her gaze at him. "You will change your mind soon enough, I am certain of it. You just need reminding..." She stepped toward him and gave a little cry, collapsing forward and splaying her hands upon his chest.

When he tried to step away, she followed him, nearly falling and forcing him to grab her arms.

"Oh no. Seem to have twisted my ankle."

Brook inhaled slowly. She was testing his patience...and his manners. His attempts to disentangle himself from her failed, and she made a whimpering sound.

"I do not think I can walk on it." She clung to him tighter.

"Perhaps if you lean..."

She whimpered when she put weight on her foot. "It is no good," she cried. "You must carry me."

He glanced at the flat ground. Either she had the weakest ankles on earth, or she was toying with him. He suspected he knew which. With a roll of his eyes, he scooped her up, not unaware of the way she beamed at him as she did so. Judith looped her arms around his neck and held herself as close as humanly possible.

His best bet was to deposit her with his mother as swiftly as possible. Brook paced his way back through the rock gardens while Judith clung tightly to him.

"This feels nice," she said, and he felt her gaze upon him.

"A twisted ankle feels nice?" he muttered, not looking down.

"No, silly, being close to you." She sighed and rested her head against him. "How perfectly we fit together."

He grimaced and marched into the formal garden then up the stairs into the house with haste. He found his mother in the parlor room, standing by the window with a cup of tea in hand. He narrowed his gaze at her as she twisted quickly and with a perfect surprised look at Judith being in his arms. She'd never tried to push him into a relationship before, even if she had murmured about wanting grandchildren soon, but Judith had done some mighty fine work.

"Oh dear, whatever happened?" his mother asked, hastening over.

"She twisted her ankle." He deposited her on the sofa with little care, sending her sprawling on the pink fabric.

"Oh." Judith swiftly righted herself, and he noticed her put pressure on her ankle before she remembered her injury.

"Well, goodness, what a shame. Perhaps you can keep her company while I send someone for some ice," his mother suggested.

"I will send someone for ice," Brook told her, exiting the room before his mother could say anything. A shudder ran through him. Even if he did not have his eyes set on Chloe, there was no chance he would marry Judith—no matter how keen his mother was on the match.

No one could compare to Chloe, and he'd do whatever he must to make her realize they were meant to be together.

Chapter Seventeen

Chloe bit back a scream. For one awful moment, she thought she had been caught. Which had been highly likely considering her plan had been extremely ill thought out. When she had realised her mother would give her no support against her father, she had hastened to Brook's house with little care for the consequences. Her father would be angry if she was, but what could be the worst that he could do? Marry her off to Mr. Lawrence immediately? She loathed arguing with her parents, but this was wrong, and her father knew it.

Of course, she did not even know where Brook's room was or if he would even be there.

So, running into him had been fortuitous indeed.

Brook gripped her arms and glanced around. "What are you doing here?"

"I needed to see you," she said breathlessly, bending double for a moment to draw breath. It was not just her hasty journey that made her lungs burn. Desperation seemed to sear her insides. Of all fates, marriage to a stranger had always seemed the worst. She had witnessed it happen to friends but never did she expect it to become her fate.

He glanced her over. "Did you run here?"

No doubt she looked as flustered and as unkempt as she felt.

His expression darkened. "What's wrong, Chlo? Has someone harmed you? By the devil, I'll— "

"No!" She pressed her palms to his chest. The instant comfort that came from feeling the strength beneath his clothing rolled through her, and she let her forehead fall against him. He rubbed a hand up and down her back, and she counted his even breaths as her own body rose and fell with them. She peered up at him, absorbing the sight of his strong jaw slightly darkened by stubble and his concerned expression.

Chloe straightened. Lord, she loved this man. How could he possibly be pretending such care? "My father...I..." She drew in a long breath. "Oh, Brook, it is terrible."

"Come with me." Keeping a grip on her arm, he led her away from the house to a secluded part of the garden, where they were surrounded by neatly trimmed box trees. A stone bench, tucked away amongst the trees, offered seclusion. Pink roses framed the nook and teased her senses with their sweet fragrance.

He motioned for her to sit. The stone bench felt cool against her heated skin. Only now did she realize how fatigued she was. Pushing a hand through his dark hair, Brook sat next to her. A peaceful hush fell over them, and Chloe appreciated the few moments to gather herself, even though she could see Brook was desperate to understand what was wrong. His tightly laced hands and fidgeting feet gave him away. Nearby, a bee dipped into a flower, and she watched it enter and retreat before twisting on the bench to face Brook.

He turned to her and brought a hand to her face, lifting her chin. A tiny thrill rushed its way through her, making her limbs feel soft and weak. Sweet Lord, she hoped he still felt *things* for her, she hoped she was not too late. She hoped she was not entirely wrong about him.

"What has happened?"

She gulped down a long breath. "My father...he wants me to marry." Her voice broke on the last word.

"I see." His tone was hollow.

"He...he found out about me spending time with you." Her chin wobbled. "He wishes me to marry Mr. James Lawrence." Chloe made a face. "He knows we would not be happy, he knows I have no desire to marry the man. But he is insisting." She shook her head. "I do not know what happened to him."

"I think I do. He would rather you be married off to some octogenarian than me."

"I do not think Mr. Lawrence is an octogenarian."

"You really want to argue with me now?"

She gave a soft chuckle and shook her head. "I really do not."

"Chloe," he looked at her intensely, "is it merely Mr. Lawrence's age that means you do not wish to marry him?"

"No," she admitted softly. "It is not just his age nor the fact I do not know the man, nor the fact that it would be an arranged marriage." She glanced at her hands. "It is because you were right."

Silence echoed between them. Above, a bird tweeted in one of the trees. The wind lightly ruffled the leaves of a grand old oak tree in front of them. Chloe risked a glance up at him to find his lips tilted in that awful, arrogant smile that made her want to swipe it from his face.

"Well, there is no need to look at me like that."

"I cannot help it. I think it is the first time you have ever admitted that I was right."

"And is that all you have to say about it?" Her heart nearly pounded out of her chest. Was he going to simply use this confession to tease her?

"No. No, it is not all I have to say about that." He shifted closer to her and cupped her face in both his hands. She closed her eyes briefly to savor the warm touch. When she opened them again, he was looking at her with more desire and love than she ever thought possible.

"Run away with me."

Chloe stared into his olive eyes. "Pardon?"

"It is a perfect solution. We elope and your father can do nothing. Our families will have no choice but to try to reconcile."

"I think you underestimate their hatred for one another," Chloe murmured. "Besides, I thought you were talking of courting me not eloping!"

"Do you want to marry that Lawrence fellow or do you want to marry me?"

She swallowed. She had not thought this far ahead. All she had considered was that she needed to tell Brook how she felt and escape her family, even for a little while. But eloping? It would bring scandal indeed and she could not be certain her father would ever talk to her again.

She could not be married to a stranger, either. She could not. Even if she did not love Brook, she could never do such a thing. If her father was angry, it would be of his own doing.

"I want to marry you," she said firmly.

A grin broke across his face. "Excellent. We shall make arrangements. If you meet me tomorrow, we can be married in Scotland within a week."

"Goodness." She felt a little breathless. "What will your family say? What if they try to disown you? What if—"

He gave her a swift peck on the lips. "All will work out, I promise. My father is not likely to disown his only son, no matter what."

She nodded slowly, trying to process the enormity of the decision they had just made. It would be a difficult deed even if their parents liked one another. To go against them like this had to be about the wildest thing she had ever done.

"I will look after you, Chloe. No matter what. I promise. You will never have to do anything you do not wish to do."

His words were like a thick blanket, wrapping around her. Suddenly she felt safe and secure. So long as she had Brook at her side, they could face almost anything.

She smiled gratefully and touched his jawline, feeling the stubble coming up from a long day. The freedom to touch him so made her smile widen. "Are you certain about this?" she asked, praying that he did not change his mind. However, she was no fool. She never went into anything without analyzing it first and the rational part of her mind could not help but want to ask these questions.

"More certain than I have ever been of anything else before."

Releasing a breath, she stroked her thumb across his jaw. "You do realize, if you marry me, you would be stuck with me forever."

"I certainly hope so."

"And you do realize, that we are quite different people. I am no good at balls and the like."

"We are different people. I realize that." He took her hand. "I know all about you, Chloe. You are clever, and kind, and determined, and absolutely perfect for me. I will admit to being no perfect gentleman in my previous life—though I will state that most of the rumors about me were utterly exaggerated—but when I'm with you, all I want to do is steal away to those libraries with you. I could not give a fig about balls and dancing and socializing when I'm with you, Chlo."

"In truth?"

He plucked a rose from the nearby bush and gave her a look. "Have I ever lied to you?"

She shook her head. He might be roguish and he certainly had the past of a rake but he had never lied to her.

"I love you." He squeezed her hands. "I will do whatever I need to prove that to you."

"You do not need to do anything." Her lungs felt tight with excitement. "I love you too," she confessed quickly before her courage vanished.

Brook offered her the rose. She took it, holding it loosely in her palms. He leaned into her, pressing warm lips against her forehead. "I love you," he repeated on a whisper.

A tremor ran through Chloe. His presence set her pulse to racing.

If her father caught him here, she didn't doubt he'd shoot him on sight.

Shaken by the thought, Chloe rested her head on his shoulder. "We'll really elope?" she asked.

"We'll go to Scotland," he said, taking her hand in his. His thumb lightly caressed the back of her hand. "Old Mr. Lawrence will not reach us there."

"But my father could," Chloe said.

"Only if he knew where we went," Brook reminded her. "Which he won't."

Chloe lifted her head and turned her gaze to his. He gave her a crooked smile, his eyes darting to her lips. "You remember the cupboard?" he asked softly.

She nodded. She could never forget the searing ache he'd left her with that kiss he'd bestowed on her. Even now, simply remembering the kiss made her stomach twist and buckle with anticipation. She had found herself remembering his touches, picturing his face, letting him occupy her every waking hour in her mind. But was she really going to do this? Marry Brook and risk disappointing her family?

He brushed back a free strand of her red hair and tucked it behind her ear. "You are the most gorgeous creature I have ever laid eyes on," he murmured. He placed a tender kiss on her right cheek. "And the most intelligent." He kissed her left cheek. "And kind." Her forehead. "And determined." He laughed, his breath tickling her face.

Chloe smirked. "What makes you say that?"

Brook pulled back, but only slightly. Their noses were almost touching. "You know what you want, and you go after it."

She feared to breathe, lest she blow him away and make him change his mind. "What do I want?" she whispered.

"Love," he answered immediately. "Even if it's forbidden."

He moved in, his lips parting as they found hers. A burst of pleasure soared through her being. She kissed him back, hoping her lips were as soft as his.

His kiss engulfed her. Any concerns fled. This was right...it was just so right. How could anything that felt like this be wrong? Somehow, by some miracle, they belonged together. She felt she was part of him, two souls yearning for the other. She couldn't stand the chaste kisses any longer.

Chloe slid her hand up his neck, twining her fingers in his downy curls and pressing her chest against his, arching her back.

Brook's breathing hitched. He wrapped both arms around her, one tight across her shoulders, the other pressing at her lower back, coaxing her closer.

The kissing sped up. His lips expertly moved across hers, eliciting passion and excitement in Chloe. Abruptly, Brook pulled away, keeping her held tightly against him. His gaze flitted across her face, his eyebrows pulling together in desperation.

"You do not make it easy on a man," he breathed. "Chlo, you are driving me to the edge of madness. I cannot wait to make you mine."

Chloe's heart hammered against her breastbone. "Then it shall be," she said, breathless from the kiss. "From this moment on, we are never to be parted."

"We'll leave for Scotland tomorrow."

"Truly?" she asked, a mix of terror and excitement bursting through her chest. She would not have to marry Mr. Lawrence and she would be with the man she loved. This handsome, charming, funny, wonderful man. She could hardly believe it.

"Truly." A smile broke across his features, and the next moment his lips had crushed against hers again. This time, he lifted her into his lap, sidesaddle. She pressed herself against him, feeling dominant now that she was slightly higher up than he. Her hands wandered everywhere they could reach—the back of his neck, his shoulders, his lower back. She scraped a trail along his spine, eliciting a low sound from his throat.

All fears of her father's hatred for his family left her. The image of standing next to old Mr. Lawrence at the church altar dissipated from her mind. In this moment, it was only her and Brook, fixed together the way they were meant to be.

A gasp escaped her throat when his hand wandered to her thigh, grasping firmly at her flesh. Chloe responded by moving her hands to his chest, trailing them down to his stomach and reveling in the solid feel of him.

Brook shuddered and quickly pulled away. "Do not tempt me, Chloe," he said with a breathless laugh. "I'm afraid you've caught me with my defenses down." He gently slid her from his lap. She pulsed with burning desire but began to cool as he scooted away from her, chuckling.

"I don't think you realize quite what a temptress you are," he said, meeting her gaze. She still saw the flames flickering in the green depths.

She opened her mouth to tell him he shouldn't have stopped, that she would have welcomed whatever it was he had wanted to do, but her blood ran cold when she heard the garden gate open and close.

Brook leapt to his feet. He took her hand in his and gave her a quick kiss. "Scotland tomorrow. Meet me at the fountain at midday."

Before she could respond, he had disappeared through the rose garden.

Chapter Eighteen

"Where are you off to?"

Brook paused by the open door of the dining room. Hunched over a newspaper with a monocle pressed to one eye, his father sat in the room alone. Though he was regaining his strength, it seemed to take him a long time to finish meals at present. Like a knife to the chest, the guilt struck. He shoved it aside. He would be back in a few weeks and would send a letter while he was on the road to Scotland so his parents knew not to worry. How his father would react to the news that he and Chloe were married, he did not know but he was willing to wager it would not be favorably.

But what were his options? Watch the woman he loved married off to a man twice her age? He'd vowed he would protect Chloe and if that meant eloping, that was what he would do. He only hoped his father survived the shock.

And, once they had grown used to the idea, perhaps both fathers could make amends. Maybe Brook was being too optimistic but he hoped in time, their marriage would bring the families together.

"Well?" his father demanded.

"Just into town, Father." Brook moved away from the door but his father called to him.

Entering the dining room fully, Brook remained standing. If he waited too long, Chloe would be there without him and might think he wasn't going to turn up.

"I met that Judith woman the other day." His father placed the monocle on the table. "Nice girl. Quite attractive."

"Indeed," he murmured vaguely.

"Your mother is terribly keen on her."

"Really? I had not noticed."

His father folded both hands across his stomach. "Far be it for me to interfere in your life, but your mother has been pressing me to ask for your thoughts on her. Apparently she would make a fine wife."

Brook grimaced. Not only would he be disappointing his father but it seemed his mother too. "She's not for me, Father."

"Oh?" He leaned back in his chair and eyed him. "She comes from good family, does she not?"

"Yes."

"What's not to like then? Easy on the eye and quite charming." He wagged a finger at him. "It is about time you married. Then you'd spend less time dancing with women like that Larkin girl."

"I have no intention of marrying Mrs. Somerset," Brook said firmly.

"I won't be around forever. Once you inherit, you'll need a good woman by your side."

Brook lifted a brow. "Were you not telling me you weren't going anywhere anytime soon the other day?"

"Well, yes," his father blustered, "but you could still do with a wife." He sighed. "I only speak of this because I want the best for you. And, well, your mother seems to think Judith is the best for you."

"She really is not, Father. I promise you that much. If I were to marry, there are many, many women far better than her."

He nodded slowly. "I trust your judgement though whether your mother will accept it, I do not know. But I did my job and asked. Hopefully she will cease nagging me now."

"Hopefully," Brook murmured, knowing that any nagging would be pointless once he returned. If his mother wanted him to find a wife, she'd be in for quite a surprise soon enough.

"She cannot say I did not try." His father retrieved the monocle and picked up his paper once more.

Brook resisted the urge to say anything more. He wanted to remind his father he loved him and wanted to make him proud but he'd likely suspect something was wrong. He only hoped his father forgave him eventually and that his marriage to Chloe really could mend bridges between the families.

The carriage awaited him outside the house. He'd packed a bag surreptitiously into the compartment, rather than have it tied to the outside to save suspicion. As yet the driver did not know he was to travel all the way to Scotland as he daren't risk word getting out, but he'd reward the man handsomely for his troubles.

A lone carriage waited by the fountain once he arrived. He didn't recognize it so it could not be Chloe but he imagined she would walk anyway. He grimaced. If only he could drive boldly up to her house and collect her rather than making her come on foot.

"Wait here," he ordered the driver once he climbed out. He glanced around the fountain area but there was no sign of her yet. A lad selling newspapers shouted out the news while a young woman sold hot crumpets at the other end of the fountain area. The gentle splashing sound of the water should have been soothing but instead he found it irritating, every plop of water setting his teeth on edge.

A few people wandered through but what felt like an eternity passed with no sign of Chloe. Lord, perhaps she had changed her mind. Surely she would not choose that Lawrence chap over him. After all her words of love too?

No, the woman loved him, he was certain of that. He'd known it even before she had. There would be a reasonable explanation for the delay.

Hands clasped behind his back, he paced around the fountain several times before pausing and pulling out his pocket watch. Blast, it had only been ten minutes. Waiting for Chloe was beginning to feel like an eternity.

He did another loop then paused, his heart near dropping into his boots. What the devil was she doing here? Had she sent out sniffer dogs or something to find him? This was getting beyond ridiculous.

Judith bounded over to him, her smile wide. He noted there was no sign of a limp.

"What luck," she said with a smile. "It must be fate that we should meet here."

"I see your ankle is healed," he murmured dryly.

"My ankle? Oh, yes, quite." She offered a hasty smile. "I heal quickly. I'm from strong stock you see."

He looked around again for any sign of Chloe. If Judith saw them leaving together she would surely make a scene or run off to his mother. Of course, his parents would have to find out eventually, but he rather wanted to give them a head start.

"Are you waiting for someone?"

"No," he said quickly.

"Well, perhaps you can accompany me for some tea. It looks to be turning into a warm day and refreshment would not hurt."

"No, thank you."

"I could keep you company," she suggested.

"No." He clenched his jaw. His manners were leaving him rapidly. Judith needed to understand his lack of interest—fast.

"It seems terribly boring just standing here. Whatever are you waiting for? It must be someone, surely?" She tilted her head. "Are you trying to keep a secret from me?"

He fixed her with a stare. "Judith, whether I am meeting someone or not is really none of your business."

"Oh, Brook, you really should consider making it my business." She lifted her chin. "I will not be dissuaded, you know. I understand that giving up one's bachelor lifestyle can be daunting but we would work so perfectly together, and I could keep you very, very happy." She shifted closer and trailed a finger down his chest. "You would hardly remember your days as a single gentleman once you have me in your bed."

He grabbed her finger and thrust it back toward her. "That is not going to happen, Judith."

Her expression darkened. "If you cannot see what a fine match we would make, then I will have to do something about that."

Before Brook had registered her dramatic change in demeanor or what was about to occur, she flung herself upon him, using every bit of strength she must have to plaster her lips to his. Brook put his hands to her arms and shoved her back.

"If you think you can force me into marriage by making a scene—" He stilled, along with his heart that came to a shuddering standstill. "Damn it. Chloe."

Chloe stood by the fountain, frozen.

"Chloe." He followed after her as she turned on her heel, heading back toward the country lane. She moved swiftly, her skirts swishing about her ankles and her bonnet bobbing on her head. "Chloe!" He caught up with her with Judith on his heels.

Coming in front of her, he forced her to a stop. Confusion and fury marred her expression. "I should have known," she said.

"Chloe—"

"You really do live up to your reputation." She glanced at her hands. "How foolish I was."

"Chloe, damn it, that was nothing."

"I would not say nothing," Judith said smugly, swinging her gaze between them. "Is this really who you were waiting for, Brook? This plain, little wallflower?"

Pain flittered in Chloe's pale gaze. He wanted nothing more than to draw her into his arms and tell her how beautiful he thought she was but he doubted she'd be receptive to that.

"I think I should go," Chloe said, the words barely a whisper.

"You damn well should not," he said. "Not until we have talked about this."

Chloe looked to Judith. "I am not sure there is anything to talk about."

"No, there isn't," Judith agreed. "Now, run along, little wallflower."

Brook curled a fist at this side. "There is plenty to talk about," he said through gritted teeth. "You know how I feel about you, Chloe. There is no need to be angry."

"No need to be angry?" she spluttered. "We were to...and you were..." She gestured to Judith. "I think I have plenty to be angry about."

Judith smiled smugly. "Do not be upset, dear. He is only a man after all."

"Judith!" Brook snapped. "Go away. I have no desire to speak to you or talk to you or even be vaguely in your presence again."

Judith's expression soured. "All because of this wallflower? This is ridiculous, Brook, you know how wonderfully we go together." Her lips curved. "How magical we are in bed."

Chloe sucked in a breath.

"Judith. Leave. At once," he ordered.

Judith huffed and barged bodily past Chloe, knocking into her with her shoulder. Chloe staggered back a few steps and rubbed her shoulder. Brook went to hold her but she backed away a few steps.

"Judith is a vindictive, spoiled brat used to getting her own way," he explained. "I had no idea she would be here nor did I wish to kiss her."

Chloe eyed him for a few moments, still massaging her shoulder. "You were lovers?"

"Once. It was a mistake."

She pressed her lips together and rubbed the end of her slightly freckled nose. "She is very attractive."

"I want you, Chlo. No one else."

Her gaze searched his. "But how can I know? How can I ever know?" She pressed a hand to her forehead. "You know, for a moment, I thought you were doing it out of revenge...that this whole plot had been to humiliate me—a Larkin."

"You really think I would do something like that?"

"I do not know," she said softly.

"Damn it, Chloe, I might be a few things but I am no heartless bastard." He could hardly believe she thought so poorly of him.

"This was a mistake." She turned away and he took her shoulder.

She shirked away from his touch. "I'm going home," she declared, lifting her chin.

"No, you are not. We're going to Scotland."

"You may go to Scotland if you wish. I am certainly not going anywhere."

"Do you really believe I intended for Judith to come here and kiss me all as some sort of a plan?"

"No...yes...no, I do not know." She opened her palms. "Do you not see? That is the problem. I do not know. How can I?" She gestured between them. "She is right about us. I am a little, plain wallflower and you are a...a handsome rogue. How can we ever have a future together?"

Coldness seeped through him, settling deep into his heart. She really did see him as nothing more than a culmination of gossip and his reputation. Apparently, his actions could not speak louder than the words of others.

"For a smart woman, Chloe, you can be incredibly foolish."

She opened her mouth then closed it for a moment. "Well, for a supposed charming gentleman, you can be incredibly rude."

"You really are a typical Larkin. So stubborn and pig-head-ed."

"And you are a typical Waverley, thinking he can have what-ever and whoever he wants." She folded her arms. "Well, you are not having me."

"Perhaps I damn well do not want you anymore!" The words escaped him before he could stop them. As soon as they were out and he saw the hurt crease her brow, he wished he could summon them back. Of course he wanted her. More than ever. He just could not believe she truly doubted him, and his high hopes for the day were being dashed swiftly like a ship on the rocks. Hope was splintering and his happiness was drowning.

"I think I shall return home now," she said quietly.

"Chloe..."

"Good day, Mr. Waverley."

"Chloe, please."

"Do not follow me." She straightened her shoulders and turned away.

He watched her walk down the lane until she vanished. Though he considered chasing her, he wasn't sure what he could possibly say. He'd just told the woman he loved he did not want her. What the devil was wrong with him? And apparently she still did not trust him. Lord, that dug deep like a knife to the chest. Maybe she was right. This had been a big mistake. Perhaps if they had been able to court openly they would have realised it sooner. A Waverley and a Larkin could never be together.

Chapter Nineteen

A knock at her bedroom door roused Chloe from her distracted state. She had a book in hand but had neglected to read a word of it, instead staring at the ceiling, wondering where on earth it went all wrong. She shut the book and sat up, shoving her hair from her face.

Someone knocked again. She cleared her throat. "Come in." The words sounded too feeble for her liking.

The door eased open and her father eased his head around the gap, not fully stepping into the room. "May I, uh, come in?"

She hardly wanted to look at him at present but she had no energy left in her to fight with her father. For all she cared, he could ditch her on boring old Mr. Lawrence. She couldn't feel anything about it. She just felt...numb.

He stepped in and closed the door gently behind him. His hands clasped behind his back, he glanced around the room and made an odd noise in his throat. Chloe eyed him expectantly.

"Your mother wanted me to tell you that your friends are here."

Her friends? Lord, she had completely forgotten their plans to meet and walk into town. She considered her likely bedraggled appearance and how little energy she had. How could she face such a thing?

"I will be down in a moment," she promised quietly. She owed her friends an explanation at least for cancelling on them.

He turned then stopped, coming back to face her. "Also, um, Chloe...about that thing..."

"Thing?"

"The, um, marriage thing."

"Yes?"

He peered at his feet. "I was mistaken."

"Oh."

A bushy brow rose. "I thought you would be happy."

"No, I am, Papa. Thank you."

He nodded. "Good. Excellent." He moved to the door. "Well then. Enjoy your time with your friends."

She forced a smile and waited until her father left the room before she let it drop. Well, that was good news she supposed. She would not have to marry Mr. Lawrence after all. And that meant it did not matter that she had not eloped with Brook.

That was a good thing, was it not?

So why did she feel so awful?

With leaden feet, she made her way downstairs to find Joanna and Augusta in the entranceway.

Joanna's brows rose when she saw her. "Chloe?"

"Joanna?"

Augusta came to her side, drawing her through into the parlor room with a gentle hand to her arm. "Whatever is the matter?"

Chloe allowed herself to be maneuvered into a chair and glanced from woman to woman. She felt awful for forgetting their plans. In truth, she had forgotten everything except Brook.

Lord, how that name sent a dart to her heart. She sniffed and pressed a hand to her chest in a bid to relieve some of the ache there. How silly of her. It would take a lot more than that to ease the pain there. She had finally taken a risk and it had failed most spectacularly. If only she had trusted her initial instincts about Brook, she could have saved herself this pain. They could never have made a successful match. Why oh why did she think a wallflower and a rogue could work together. She sniffed again and tried to swallow the aching knot in her throat, but it would not shift.

"Chloe?" Joanna tried again, sinking down next to her, ever beautiful, even in her crepe mourning dress, while Chloe felt like a tangled mess in her most comfortable muslin gown and her hair messy from trying to rub away the burgeoning headache that had been plaguing her all morning.

"I forgot we were meeting today." She gave a weak smile.

"What has happened?" Augusta pressed.

"Oh nothing really. I was just intending to elope with Mr. Waverley." She took Augusta's offered handkerchief and dabbed at her sore eyes. "Nothing of importance."

"Elope?" Joanna spluttered. "Why would you do such a thing?"

"My father wishes me to marry someone else. Or at least he did." Chloe scrunched the handkerchief in both hands. "I was feeling a little desperate you see."

Augusta shook her head. "Oh, Chloe, why did you not tell us?"

Chloe stared at the balled-up piece of fabric, the A for Augusta peeking out between her fingertips. "I am not certain. And it happened very quickly."

"We are your friends," Joanna reminded her. "We could have helped or at least offered advice."

Nodding numbly, Chloe glanced between her two friends. She'd only had them as companions for a little while and, truth be told, they were the first true female friends she had ever had. It was hard to know what to do with them at times.

"You are right," Chloe said on a sigh. "If I had taken but a moment to confide in you, I would have saved myself this pain and humiliation."

"What happened?" Augusta asked softly.

"We were to elope to Scotland today." The words sounded silly and hollow when she said them aloud. "Or at least that is what I thought. But it seems Brook was living up to his reputation."

"How so?" Joanna pressed.

"When I arrived to meet him, he was with another woman." When she pictured him with the beautiful, raven-haired woman, the pain in her chest started anew. "They were kissing," she added.

Augusta gasped.

"Oh dear," Joanna said.

Tears began to bite behind her eyes again and Chloe dropped her face into her hands, her cheeks burning. She felt small and silly and ridiculous all at the same time. The one time she did something frivolous and she wound up with a broken heart. How very typical.

A few moments of silence passed and Chloe lifted her head to see both women exchanging looks.

"What happened after that? What did he say?" Augusta asked softly.

"The woman—Judith I think it was—said they had been lovers for some time." Chloe grimaced. "She was so beautiful."

"Did you speak to Brook?" Joanna asked.

"Of course." Chloe's chest hurt anew. "We argued. He denied it all and could not believe I doubted him. But you should have seen them together. They looked so"—she gestured with open palms, bringing them together— "perfect with one another."

Joanna pressed her lips together. "Did you believe him? That they were not lovers?"

"I-I'm not certain. Either way, it does not matter. How could I have ever thought we could be together? Even if he is not guilty of such a thing, it is clear I am not able to get past my doubts. What sort of relationship could we have?"

Joanna leaned over and squeezed her bunched hands. "What can we do for you?"

Biting down on her bottom lip, Chloe lifted both shoulders. It was not terribly conducive at the moment but mostly she wanted to curl up in a ball and cry until there were no more tears left. She could not decide if it was over Brook, because she was so embarrassed, or because she hated herself for letting her fears get the better of her.

"I think...I had better take some time for myself. I am not good company at present."

Joanna nodded her understanding, but Augusta peered at her closely. "Are you certain? We can stay for as long as you need."

"She needs to be alone for a while," Joanna said, standing.

Chloe smiled gratefully Joanna. If anyone could understand the pain of losing someone, it was her. Not that Chloe would compare her agony to Joanna's.

Augusta and Joanna promised to visit tomorrow though Chloe could not see things looking any brighter then. Even with her father less inclined to marry her off.

"Chloe," called her mother.

Standing, she straightened her dress and swiped at her eyes. The last thing she needed was her mother asking questions. She could never admit how deeply she had fallen for Brook now that it was all over.

Her mother popped her head around the drawing room door. "Is that your bag in the hallway?"

Chloe grimaced. She must have dropped it there in her haste to get inside. It contained all the things she needed for a trip to Scotland.

"Oh, yes, that is mine. Forgive me. Joanna and Augusta arrived early and I forgot all about it."

"Whatever did you need such large bag for?"

Chloe scooted past her mother and snatched up the bag in question, holding it close to her chest. "Um...books of course."

Her mother rolled her eyes. "Of course."

"I...I had better go and put them away."

"Chloe—" her mother started, but Chloe dashed upstairs before anything else could be said.

In her bedroom, she unbuckled the bag and dumped her belongings onto the bed. Eyeing the crumpled mess, her nose tingled. She sniffed away the beginning of another deluge of tears and snatched an armful of clothes.

Wrenching open the armoire, she jolted. "What on earth are you doing in there?"

Freddie peered up at her, his freckled face creased as he blinked in the light. He had a book in one hand and a candle in the other. Leaning forward, he glanced around. "Are you alone?" His gaze narrowed. "Have you been crying?"

"Of course not. And yes I am alone. Why? Are you in trouble?"

"No. I do not think so." He waved the book at her. "At least, not yet."

"Not yet?"

He eased himself out of the piece of furniture and slid to the floor, then blew out the candle and put it on the side table. "I do not think Mama would like it if I read this." He sniggered. "It is a bit naughty."

"Naughty?" She snatched the book off him, ignoring his protests. "Where on earth did you find a naughty book?"

"Up in the attic." He tried to take it off her but she held it aloft. He jumped twice then folded his arms when he failed to grab the book, his lips forming a pout. "Give it back, I found it, it's mine."

Chloe glanced at the cover. Dusty and faded in places, it was thinner than a normal book and had faint gold writing on the front that was mostly rubbed off. She squinted at it. The indent read 'diary.' "This is most definitely not yours. Is this Mama's?"

Her little brother made a face. "Lord, no. I would certainly not be reading it if it was. That would be disgusting."

Flicking it open, her gaze landed immediately on some rather explicit details, written in delicate handwriting that surely had to be a woman's. It was certainly not the sort of content her brother should be reading about, but she could see why he was so captivated. She turned to the first page and sucked in a breath. "Julia," she murmured.

Freddie nodded. "I do not know who she is. I want to know how her diary ended up here."

Chloe knew. She guessed that Freddie had not considered the man talked about in the diary might be his father. That was probably for the best.

"Should you not be getting to your studies? I would wager your governess is waiting for you."

He crossed his eyes and stuck his tongue out. "Studies are boring. That is much more interesting."

"I am sure it is, but it is not really suitable for you."

"Oh, Chloe, why do you have to spoil my fun? I would never have showed you if I'd realised you'd be so boring about it."

Shooing him out of her bedroom, she kept the book out of his reach. "Sometimes older sisters have to spoil their little brother's fun. It is part of the job description."

"But—"

Chloe shut the door on him before he could protest and turned the key in the lock. Sinking onto the bed amongst her crumpled clothes, she opened the diary and began to read. Once it reached the more graphic moments, she skipped past those. There was nothing there she needed to know—or wanted to know. However, it soon became clear that there was information both the Waverleys and the Larkins should be aware of. Now she understood why Brook's father had a different story to tell about Julia.

It seemed the woman was in love with both men.

My heart is torn. Both are excellent men, of equal standing, and treat me with nothing less than great respect. When I am with George, my heart soars, and when I am with Marcus, I feel things I did not think humanly possible. Part of me thinks I should run away and deny myself any happiness ever rather than make a choice. But if I do, we shall all be unhappy. Is it right to make two people happy and one very miserable? I suppose only time will tell.

By the time Chloe had nearly finished reading, the room had grown dark. She had failed to draw the curtains and quiet dusk settled over the gardens, turning it a shade of blue-gray. Her neck was stiff from being hunched over the diary and when she put a hand to it and tilted her head from side to side, she felt it crick. The dinner gong echoed through the house. She grimaced. She just needed a few more moments.

Lighting a candle, she rushed through the last few pages. She was beginning to understand why her father and Mr. Waverley adored Julia so much. She seemed a clever and kind woman. Her chest grew heavy and tight when she landed on the last page. Julia knew she was dying and was aware she had created even more of the rift between the families.

If I could see but one thing before I go, it would be George and Marcus enjoying one another's company once more.

Chloe blinked away budding tears and carefully shut the book. Both men needed to know this. Surely, if they loved Julia as much as Julia had spoken of, they would make peace with one another.

Chapter Twenty

"That bloody woman." Brook paced past the fireplace and back again.

Benedict watched him from his seat, saying little. Elizabeth stood behind her husband, a hand resting on his shoulder while she eyed Brook. He couldn't face another day at home with his parents questioning why he looked like he was ready to attack someone.

It was because his foolish past had caught up with him. Because he'd argued with Chloe and flung accusations at her rather than talked it through. Because he feared he'd lost her forever and had little idea how to fix this.

But he could say none of that, so his next best bet had been to escape to Benedict's.

The scent of coffee lingered in the air, but he hadn't drunk a drop. Coming here and burdening his friends with this was a mistake perhaps but it was certainly not a matter he could discuss with his father and Lord knew, he was making a hash of it on his own.

Brook paused and scowled at Elizabeth's slightly amused look. "What is it?"

She gave a half-smile. "Forgive me, but I never thought I would see you in such a tangle over a woman."

He shoved a hand through his hair. "Well, she is quite a woman."

"So it seems," Benedict said. "You must be absurdly in love if you were willing to give up your bachelor lifestyle and elope."

"I would not say *absurdly* in love." Brook grimaced. Perhaps it was absurdly so. If he was willing to upset his family and risk their ire, he most certainly had to be madly, deeply, absurdly in love.

"Well, what are you going to do about it?" demanded Elizabeth. "You are not going to let that vile Judith ruin things, are you?"

Elizabeth knew Judith from London and they had never been friends, so she did not appear at all surprised when Brook explained what had happened.

Shaking his head, Brook sighed. He couldn't let Judith win. But to get to Chloe, he would have to trespass on Larkin land with a high chance of getting shot if he did so. He could wait until nightfall and do as he has done before but he very much doubted Chloe would entertain the thought of sneaking out to see him. The problem was, he hardly blamed her. With his past, was it any wonder she thought the worst of him?

Well, Chloe had to leave her house at some point. She could not remain hidden away there forever. As soon as she stepped off Larkin land, he would take his chance and try to explain, with infinitely more eloquent words, what had happened.

"If I were you, Brook, I would waste no time, whatever you are going to do." Elizabeth moved to the side table and poured a cup of coffee, turning and taking a sip. "Did I not hear that she was to marry Mr. Lawrence?"

Brook made a face. "She will never marry him."

"Unfortunately as women, we often have no choice. Her mother was suggesting they were going to see him today, I believe. Mr. Larkin is known for being soft on his daughter, so I should imagine Mr. Lawrence wishes to get the marriage contract drawn up quickly before her father changes his mind."

A chill ran through him. Brook curled a fist at his side. He'd been so damn wrapped up in the idea of them eloping, he'd forgotten the real reason they had even agreed to speed things up. He couldn't let Chloe marry that old stick of a man.

"I need to get to her."

Benedict nodded. "I think you do."

Mr. Larkin could shoot him for all he cared, he had to get to Chloe. He bid Benedict and Elizabeth a hasty farewell and retrieved his horse from the stables, cutting a swift path toward the Larkin estate. Perhaps Elizabeth was incorrect and Chloe was not due to visit with Lawrence today. Maybe Mr. Larkin had even changed his mind. None of it mattered, he needed to see Chloe and he needed to see her now.

Bunching the reins tight in his hand, the leather strips cut into his palms. He should have risked being shot in the first place and followed her and insisted they made up immediately. He could think of many, many better ways of ending that argument, but his foolish pride had got the better of him.

He slowed the horse when he spied a carriage thundering along the road from the Larkin estate. He was some distance away still but he recognized the carriage as Chloe's fathers. His heart beat a sickening tattoo against his chest. They were going to Lawrence's—they had to be.

And he was going to lose Chloe forever.

He urged the horse into action. If they moved fast enough, he could intercept the carriage and force Chloe to listen to him. Who knew if her father was with them—he might end up being beaten to a bloody pulp—but it would be worth it if he could only tell Chloe the truth.

He loved her even if they fought. Even if it took him an eternity to prove himself to her. He'd wait forever if he had to. So long as she didn't marry that man.

Trees whipped at his face, the sting hardly registering while he rode down a path seldom travelled. With any luck, it would bring him out in front of the carriage. His pulse beat hard in his ears and he could feel his blood rush through his veins—hot and urgent. Every instinct in his body urged him to get to her. He'd promised to protect her at all costs and if he did not prevent her from marrying a man she did not know, he would no longer be doing his job.

"Good girl," he urged the horse, breaths coming fast as they emerged onto the road. He cursed when he spied the carriage, bumping its way along the country road up ahead. "Looks like we're not done yet, girl." With a flick of the reins, he continued his pursuit.

Coming alongside of the carriage, he was all too aware of the driver noting his presence and flexing his hand at his side. It was likely he travelled with a pistol in case they ran into highwaymen. He'd risk getting shot if he had to, but he'd rather not end up with a hole in his chest.

"I need to talk to Miss Larkin," he called to the driver.

The man shook his head, glancing him over. The chances were he thought it a trick to get him to stop. Brook did not blame him. Highwaymen were known to pretend to be in trouble to force carriages to a halt.

"I'm Mr. Brook Waverley," he said, keeping pace with the carriage. "You must know me."

"Even if you are, you will have to wait," the man shouted back. "We are late as it is."

"It is an urgent matter!"

The driver shrugged and turned his attention back to the road. Damn it. As much as he was glad the Larkin's driver was a cautious man, well capable to taking care of Chloe, he'd hoped it would not come to this.

He propelled the horse forward, ensuring there was a large gap between him and the carriage before dismounting and tethering his mount to a tree at the side of the road. The carriage bore down upon him, the horse's hooves making the ground vibrate. Brook swallowed and tugged at this collar. The man wouldn't risk running over a Waverley...would he?

Palm out, Brook held his ground. The driver waved his hand frantically, motioning for him to move aside. Brook planted his feet firmly, his shoulders squared. This was going to hurt a great deal if the driver did not slow down soon enough.

The gap between them closed. The horses neared. The vibrations of the wheels and hooves pounding the ground rumbled up through his limbs. Brook half-closed his eyes and braced himself for the impact.

A whinny of horses and the uncomfortable screech of a carriage rocking on its suspension, and the driver brought it to a halt, a mere foot or so from Brook. He felt the hot breath of the horses on his face.

"You bloody idiot," the driver shouted. "Do you want to die."

"Not particularly," Brook quipped, "but I do thank you, sir, for not crushing me to death."

The carriage door opened and Mr. Larkin popped his head out. "What the devil is going on?" His gaze landed on Brook. "What are *you* doing here?"

Hands held up in surrender, Brook took a few steps back as Mr. Larkin stepped out of the carriage and stalked toward him. He should have guessed Chloe would be travelling with both parents.

"Mr. Larkin, I just wish to have a word with your daughter," Brook tried.

"You will do nothing of the sort. You will stay far away from her." Chloe's father thrust a finger out at him and moved closer. "What the devil sort of game are you playing? Get out of here before I shoot you."

"Just a brief word, Mr. Larkin, I promise."

"Johnson, hand me your gun." Mr. Larkin gestured to the driver who reluctantly handed over what was likely to be a loaded pistol.

Brook lifted his hands higher. "I do not want trouble."

Chloe's father aimed the gun at Brook's chest. "You Waverleys are always trouble."

"What is going on?" came a soft voice. Chloe's mother, elegant in dark red with a high collar, stood by the carriage. "Marcus, why are you trying to shoot Mr. Waverley?"

"Mr. Waverley?" Chloe leaped from the vehicle, her eyes wide.

Brook might well have been shot in the chest for all he knew. Seeing her made his entire body hurt. In a delicate pale green gown, overlaid with a sheath of lace and her hair coiled delicately up with sprigs of curls around her face, she looked every inch the bride to be. He clenched his jaw. He didn't want her looking beautiful for that bloody Lawrence. He wanted her beautiful for *himself.*

"Get out of here, Waverley, before I do something we both regret," Mr. Larkin spat.

"I am sorry, sir, but I cannot." He glanced over at Chloe. "I must speak with your daughter."

"I'll kill you first."

Brook looked into Mr. Larkin's pale gaze. He might be aged but his hand was steady, and Brook did not doubt the man would follow through on his threat.

"I am not moving," Brook insisted. "I cannot you see." He looked past the man to Chloe. "You can't marry Lawrence, Chlo," he said. "I won't let it happen."

"But, Brook—" Chloe took a step forward and stilled when her father whirled on her.

"Brook?" he spluttered.

"You can't marry him because I want to marry you," Brook said, using her father's distraction to step to the side, away from the gun. "I want to marry you, Chloe. Even if you do not trust me yet. Even if I have to court you for endless years. Even if your father wants to shoot me."

Chloe's lips curved slightly.

"I love you, Chlo. I always will. Even if you hate me. But you cannot marry a man you do not know. You just cannot."

"Damn it, Waverley."

Out of the corner of his eye, Brook saw the gun lift again.

"Papa, no!" Chloe raced forward, placing herself between the gun and Brook.

Mr. Larkin's eyes widened and he swiftly lowered the pistol. "Good God, Chloe, would you really align yourself with this man?"

She nodded. "I would." She reached behind her and took Brook's hand.

He tried and failed not to grin like a fool and wound his fingers between hers.

"I love him, Papa. I very much wish to marry him." She turned around, a smile stretching lips that he'd kill to taste. "I love you. And I do trust you. I am sorry I ever let my doubts get the better of me." She shook her head. "Those doubts were not about you but about myself. Whether I could really keep a man like you interested. But you have never made me feel anything less than worthy."

He groaned. "You are more than worthy. In fact, it is I who is unworthy of you." He took both her hands in his. "But I will spend the rest of my days proving myself to you."

"Chloe," her father spluttered. "You cannot be serious."

She turned back to her father. "I am, Papa. He is a good man, you will see."

"No." He shook his head vigorously. "He's a Waverley, nothing can change that."

"Actually something can." Chloe tugged a book from under her pelisse. "This can."

Mr. Larkin frowned. "What is that?"

"It is about Julia," Chloe said softly.

"Julia..." her father murmured, his cheeks paling rapidly.

Brook eyed the small, tattered book but had little idea what it was and why it pertained to the woman their fathers had fought over. "Chloe?"

"Trust me, Brook, I think I can solve this," she said, pressing a hand to his chest. "Mama, can we go to the Waverleys' house?"

Her mother had remained frozen by the carriage, her expression a little wan. She nodded slowly. "I suppose so, dear."

"Not a chance in hell," Mr. Larkin bit out.

"For once in your life, stop being so stubborn," Chloe's mother snapped.

Chloe's father opened his mouth then closed it. He tucked the pistol into his jacket. "This does not mean I will not shoot you still." He stalked back to the carriage and was herded in by his wife.

"I hope you have something good there, Chlo. I really would rather not be shot."

She grinned. "It is very good, believe me. I am certain what is in here shall ensure our fathers do not fight again."

"Will it also ensure I can marry you?"

"I very much hope so." She bit down on her bottom lip.

"If your father were not here, I would kiss you right now."

"If my father were not here, I would kiss *you* right now," she countered.

"We shall have to save it for when your father is no longer threatening to kill me, I suppose."

"Hopefully that will be sooner rather than later." She motioned to his horse. "Will you ride on? We shall catch up with you."

"Of course."

"And, Brook...why did you chase after the carriage?"

"I couldn't let you marry Lawrence."

Chloe frowned. "I wasn't going to marry Lawrence."

"You're not? You weren't?"

"No. My father changed his mind. We were just travelling to visit with my aunt."

He grimaced. "Well, I wish I had known before I stepped in front of that carriage."

"You stepped...? Oh, Brook, you could have been killed!"

He lifted a shoulder. "Would have been worth it." He grinned. "Perhaps."

She pressed a palm to his chest. "I love you," she said shyly.

"I love you too." He glanced around and pressed the briefest of kisses to her lips, leaving her looking stunned. "You are utterly worth dying for, Chlo," he told her as he mounted his horse.

Chapter Twenty-One

"Brook, where the—" George Waverley paused, confusion crossing his brow before he bunched his fists by his sides. "Brook, fetch my shotgun. We have intruders," he growled.

Brook stepped swiftly in between the two men while Chloe's father held up his palms. "I am only here at your son's insistence."

"Before you go killing anyone, Father, I need you to listen to this." He motioned to Chloe. "Go ahead."

"I am not listening to a word that comes out of a Larkin's mouth. They are all lies!" Mr. Waverley took a step forward but Brook blocked his father from coming any closer.

"Perhaps we should go, dear," Chloe's mother said, hooking her arm through her father's and moving to tug him away.

In the close confines of the entryway, surrounded by tall marble pillars, Chloe could well understand her mother's concern. Despite his recent illness, Mr. Waverley was a large-set man with a hard gaze and a determined stance.

Chloe shook her head. "Please don't, Mama. We need to do this."

"Do what, though, Chloe? Anger the man? I do believe he really will shoot us," her mother murmured.

"What is all this noise?" Mrs. Waverley stepped through into the hallway and stilled at the sight of them all gathered in the room. Her eyes widened and her skin paled, making her look wan against her dark, gray-streaked hair. "Oh goodness."

"Mother, all is well," Brook assured her.

"It is not bloody well!" Mr. Waverley spluttered. "Margaret, go fetch my shotgun," he demanded.

Mrs. Waverley remained frozen, her gaze darting between them all. Chloe drew in a shaky breath. She should have known this would not be easy but she had rather hoped it would not go as far as both fathers fighting in a duel.

"If you want to shoot me, then shoot me, Waverley," her father barked. "I don't think you have the balls."

"Marcus!" Her mother clapped her hands over Chloe's ears. "Not in front of the children!"

"I've been wanting to shoot you for decades." Mr. Waverley's knuckles whitened as he gripped his cane.

"Likewise," her father shot back.

Chloe tugged her mother's hands away from her ears and stepped forward, placing herself directly in the middle of both fathers. "We will be gone in a trice," she promised Mr. Waverley, "and if you choose, you may never have to see us again. But both of you need to hear this."

"I do not need to hear any word from a Larkin's mouth." Mr. Waverley motioned to Brook with his cane. "I told you she was trouble."

"Father, just listen for once in your life." Brook put a hand to his father's cane and forced him to lower it.

"I would rather—"

"It is about Julia," Chloe said hastily.

Mr. Waverley's red cheeks paled rapidly. "What did you say?"

"Julia," her father muttered and Chloe shot a quick glance at her father to see him looking a little faint. Her mother clasped his arm tightly and gave Chloe a nod.

"I found her diary at our house," Chloe announced. "It was written from before her marriage to my father to just before her death."

"Damn you to hell, Marcus," Mr. Waverley muttered.

"I had nothing to with her death!" her father rejoined.

"Please," Chloe begged, "just listen." She flicked open the diary and began to read. "*My greatest regret will be the rift I caused between Marcus and George. They are both fine men and I wish I had the strength in me to mend their friendship. I wish I had not left it so late. My only hope is that they share their grief for me and help each other once I am gone.*"

She lifted her gaze to look at both men. A silence hung over the room, punctuated only by the muffled footsteps of a servant somewhere upstairs.

"She loved you, Papa," Chloe said softly. "And you, Mr. Waverley." She turned to Brook's father. "She did not know how to choose between you both but she followed her heart. No one was stolen from anyone but she understood how much she had hurt you, Mr. Waverley." Lifting the book, she held it out to him. "You should read this. As should you, Papa."

Mr. Waverley's chin wobbled as he gingerly took the book from her. His wife came to his side and gave his arm a squeeze. "I think perhaps both of you should take some time together. Mrs. Larkin and I can have tea with the children."

"But—"

"For Julia," Chloe said.

Mr. Waverley exhaled and eyed Chloe's father before giving a slight nod.

"Papa?" Chloe pressed.

A few heartbeats passed, no one moving a muscle.

"Marcus?" her mother prompted.

"Very well," her father finally agreed, his voice gravelly.

"Do you know Mrs. Somerset?" Mrs. Waverley asked as the two men slunk off.

Chloe shook her head, not really hearing the words as she watched her father and Mr. Waverley leave. Tension fizzed in the air and both men held their postures tight but at least they were not fighting. Lord, she hoped this was it—that this really was the end of it all. Beside her, Brook groaned, though Chloe could not fathom why. She was not ready to relax but it seemed their fathers would not kill each other, and she was convinced Julia's words would be the perfect remedy to their discord.

"Mrs. Somerset is quite delightful and happens to be having tea with me today," Mrs. Waverley continued. "I am certain you shall enjoy her company, Mrs. Larkin."

Chloe's mother smiled, though it did not quite reach her eyes. She still seemed a little stunned by the whole scenario, but Chloe was not surprised. Brook had professed his love in one of the more dramatic ways, details of her father's past had been revealed that could be uncomfortable for her mother, and they were in the Waverleys' home for the first time. Still, her mother did a fine job of nodding politely and following Mrs. Waverley through to the parlor room.

"Chloe," Brook hissed, but she ignored him in favor of appearing as polite as possible. After all, his mother did not yet know of their plans and she could not help but want to make her future mother-in-law like her.

Following the mothers into the drawing room, Chloe smiled at the elegantly designed room—trimmed with floor-length pale pink curtains and furnished with a dark wood and chairs in matching fabrics. A piano and harp sat in one corner by a drawing desk. Brook's mother clearly had excellent taste.

Her gaze landed on the unknown guest, currently seated by the fireplace. "You," she said before she could stop herself.

Judith gave a vague smile, as though she had never seen Chloe before. "I heard some shouting," Judith said sweetly. "Is all well, Mrs. Waverley?" She rose from the delicate seat on which she'd been perched and came to Mrs. Waverley's side. "I think you should sit. You look a little flushed. Why do I not—"

Brook's mother waved a hand. "I am well, I am well." She turned to Chloe and her mother. "Do you know Mrs. Larkin and Miss Larkin?"

"I do not believe—"

"Well, that's a bloody lie," muttered Brook.

"Brook!" his mother scolded.

"She knows Miss Larkin quite well, Mother, I can assure you of that. In fact, she had the audacity to lay her hands on my fiancée only the other day."

"Lay her hands...? Fiancée...?" His mother put a hand to her mouth.

Chloe winced. This was not the way she had envisaged breaking the news to Brook's family.

Her mother cleared her throat. "Perhaps we should leave Mr. Waverley and his mother to talk?" she suggested, taking Chloe's arm.

"No, I should much rather you stay here and explain this all to me," Mrs. Waverley said firmly.

Judith stood. "Well, I can see this is a family matter so I think perhaps—"

"You stay too," Brook's mother snapped.

Judith dropped swiftly onto the chair with a thump, her cheeks red. She kept her gaze lowered while Mrs. Waverley motioned for them all to sit. Chloe sat on the sofa with her mother while Brook occupied another single chair near the fireplace—the only one that looked vaguely masculine in the whole room. Mrs. Waverley remained standing.

"Mrs. Larkin, I think I must ask, did you know of this engagement?"

Her mother nodded. "But I only just found out. I was as shocked as I am sure you are."

Mrs. Waverley turned to Brook. "Tell me now, as your mother, are you sincere in this? I love you dearly, you know I do, but I am not blind to your behavior. If you are—"

Brook lifted a hand. "I am sincere, Mother." He sent a look Chloe's way. "I love Miss Larkin very much."

Chloe looked away as warmth spread up into her face. How wonderful and odd it felt to hear him declare it aloud.

"How did you two...? When did...?" Mrs. Waverley finally dropped into the chair next to Judith. "Never mind. I am not sure I wish to know."

Chloe's mother leaned over and patted the back of her hand. "I think your son and my daughter are very much in love."

Mrs. Waverley glanced between the two of them. "So it seems."

"Well, this is preposterous," Judith spluttered. "How can you love someone like her? Everyone knows what you are like, Brook. Do you really think she shall make you happy?"

Quiet muffled the room for several moments. Chloe opened her mouth but Brook spoke first. "She will. She does," he confirmed.

"But...but she's a wallflower. She's not even pretty."

"Judith," Mrs. Waverley snapped. "I expected better from you."

"Well, she isn't." Judith folded her arms across her chest and sank further into her chair.

Chloe could not even blame Judith for her words. She was no society beauty and most certainly a wallflower, but Brook made her feel beautiful every moment of every day and she did not doubt his feelings for her.

"Mrs. Waverley..." Chloe looked to her mother. "Mama, I know this is a shock and we did not intend to keep this a secret but with the disagreement between Papa and Mr. Waverley, we did not know how to tell you."

Her mother gave a light laugh. "It will be even more interesting when we tell your fathers."

Chloe made a face. "I am trying not to think of that."

"I think perhaps Mrs. Larkin and I should handle this," Mrs. Waverley suggested.

"Yes, a fine idea."

"Why don't you two go and take a little walk in the gardens? Mrs. Larkin and I can discuss how we should move forward." Mrs. Waverley made a shooing motion.

"Oh, I should probably—" Judith went to stand.

"You can stay here and explain exactly what happened when you touched my soon-to-be- daughter," Mrs. Waverley ordered.

Chloe managed to keep her smug smile to herself until they left the room and stepped out onto the veranda, blinking in the bright sunlight. The gardens stretched out in front of her, a long path cutting down the center of a carefully managed flowerbed and stone plant pots. It was the first time she'd ever seen the garden at the Waverleys and it was beautiful. She released a long breath and shared a smile with Brook.

"That could have been worse," he said.

"Yes, it really could have been."

"With any luck, that shall be the last time Judith is seen here." He took her hand. "I am still deeply sorry for what happened—that my past caught up with me."

"I hope there are no other heartbroken lovers waiting to attack me."

"Oh, only a handful," he teased, leading her down the steps into the formal gardens. Flowers teased her ankles, a beautiful array of yellows and purples. The scent wrapped around her, reminding her of their time in her own gardens, when he had proposed and, well, done other things.

"You are blushing, Chlo."

"I was just thinking of...well, it does not matter."

Brook whirled her around so that she twirled into his arms. She sighed and sank into his embrace. She had not been sure she would feel this again—his strong arms, his firm torso—supporting her and making her feel loved in a way she never thought possible. She rested her head against his chest, closed her eyes and felt his solid heartbeat—steady and reassuring.

"Do you think our fathers will become friends?" she asked.

"If not friends, then they will have no choice but to become acquaintances once we marry."

She lifted her head away from him to peer up at him. "I think our mothers will become friends."

He nodded. "I think so too."

"And now we no longer have to elope."

His lips tilted. "A shame. I was rather looking forward to doing something scandalous."

"I, for one, rather like avoiding scandal."

"Well, I hope you are ready to join me in a life of scandal, Chlo. It shall never be boring, I promise you that."

She grinned and rose on her toes to kiss him briefly. "I was counting on that."

Chapter Twenty-Two

The strains of a country dance cut through the excited buzz of chatter. The daylight faded fast with streams of amber light dappling in through the tall windows of the ballroom. Chandeliers glittered and highlighted the guests' finery. Brook shook his head to himself with a grin. It was a fine engagement ball indeed.

And Chloe was missing the whole thing.

He searched out her friends who were seated together on the edge of the dancefloor. Joanna caught his eye and gave a little shrug. None of them were surprised that Chloe had vanished.

Neither was he. But he'd be damned if he'd spend the evening without her.

Before he could stride off, his father approached with Mr. Larkin. It could not be claimed they were the best of friends yet, but both men were trying hard to mend their relationship. The end of the argument over the land had already benefited both men, who appeared less tired and a darn sight more relaxed.

"I was hoping Miss Larkin might be with you," his father said over the chatter.

Mr. Waverley grimaced. "She is probably—"

"In the library," Brook finished for her father.

Mr. Larkin chuckled. "You know her well it seems."

"We can talk more on this in the morning, but Marcus and I wished to let you and Miss Larkin know that we have decided on an engagement gift for you both."

"Uh..." Brook peered around. Now he wished Chloe was at his side. She would be much better at saying all the correct thank yous.

"We are gifting you the land." Mr. Larkin's smile widened.

Brook glanced between both fathers who appeared proud of themselves indeed. "The land?" he echoed.

"Indeed. The much-contested land." His father clasped his hands behind his back and rocked briefly on his heels. "It will be gifted with certain clauses, ensuring that it shall remain equally yours and Chloe's."

"So you see, it will be both Larkin and Waverley land." Mr. Larkin's grin grew even bigger.

"Ah."

"Ah? Is that all you can say, Son?" his father asked.

"Forgive me. It is an excellent idea." He patted his father's arm. "Thank you, I appreciate it. Hopefully I can speak for Chloe when I say she will be happy that we have a resolution too."

"We thought it a rather fine idea." Mr. Waverley shared a proud look with Brook's father.

Brook smiled and shook his head. When he'd wanted the two men to make up, he'd never anticipated they'd end up plotting together to fix centuries of discord over the land. He was only a little annoyed he had not thought of the resolution himself.

"Well, we shall leave you to your celebrations. Hopefully my daughter shall make an appearance soon."

Once both men had eased back into the crowd, Brook used the opportunity to slip through the well-wishers to the edge of the ballroom before anyone else nabbed him for conversation. He gave Elizabeth and Benedict a little wave then he headed toward the library, marching quickly until he reached the door. He eased it open and allowed himself a smile. With her head bent low over a book, her legs curled up to one side and her shoes kicked off revealing her stockings, Chloe made quite the picture. Indeed, it was a picture he had imagined many times since their engagement. He looked forward to moments like these—personal, private moments that revealed the true Chloe.

She had already surrounded herself with a few books, like a little fortress. He only hoped she would let him in.

"Oh." She lifted her head and made a face. "I am sorry, Brook. I tried very hard to remain but everyone wished to speak with me and..."

He closed the gap between them swiftly. "You do not need to apologize." He sank onto the oriental rug next to her, allowing himself a moment to admire her in the lamplight. The golden tones highlighted her red hair and softened lips that made him ache to kiss her. Rubies glinted in her ears and around her neck.

He wanted to kiss her there too.

He wanted to kiss the damned woman all over. The sooner they were married the better. Seeing her like this just reminded him how much he loved Chloe Larkin—even if she did abandon him at their own engagement ball.

"I know I should have stayed," she said softly.

"It is well enough." He took the book from her hands and laid it gently away from her so that he could shift closer and cup her face.

"I know, but—"

"Chloe, I do not mind," he insisted, stroking a thumb across her impossibly soft skin. "In fact, I confess to feeling the need to escape too."

"You did? You do?"

He nodded. "Why would I wish to be with a hundred strangers when I could be with you?"

"But you love balls!"

"I love you more."

She gave a shy smile. "Are you certain? Brook, I—I will try harder next time. I promise."

"No. Don't. Just be you, Chlo. That's all I ask."

She shook her head and leaned into his shoulder. He wrapped an arm around her and held her close for several moments, enjoying the simple intimacy of the moment. She eased away and peered up at him.

"You can go back to the ball if you wish. I do not mind. And I promise to put in an appearance before everyone leaves."

"And leave you? Like hell."

"Brook," she scolded.

"Why would I wish to dance and dine and gossip when I can be here, being scolded by you."

"Brook," she said again, tapping his arm.

"See? This is much more fun."

"Not yet it is not."

He frowned then grinned at her mischievous look. Chloe would keep him on his toes, of that he was certain. Who needed balls when he had a feisty, intelligent wallflower to keep him company?

Leaning in, he pressed a whisper-soft kiss to the corner of her lips. She inhaled sharply and wrapped her hands around his shoulders. He shifted to angle himself better, pressing more kisses along her jaw and down her neck. She tilted her head to allow him better access and he inhaled her violet scent and savored the softness of her skin. He ought to tell her about what their fathers had planned but he was fairly certain that could wait. Right now, lavishing her with attention was far more important.

He eased her back onto the rug, admiring the way her dress splayed out against the fabric and her hands rested by her head just so—waiting for him. He paused for a moment and she frowned.

"What is it?"

"I was just thinking I have to be the luckiest bastard in the world," he confessed.

She smiled softly and reached for him. "And I am the luckiest...um...woman."

He chuckled and came to lie next to her, smoothing a hand down her side so that he could feel every curve until his hand landed on the soft give of her thigh. He groaned in the back of his throat.

"The sooner we are married, the better."

"It is only a month away," she reminded him.

He pressed a kiss to the side of her face then her lips. "A month too long."

"What I mean, is it is only a month." She smoothed her hands over his shoulders. "We do not have to wait."

Brook froze and he could have sworn his heart did too. "Chlo?"

"You know what I am saying," she whispered as she wrapped her arms around his neck and drew him to her.

He stared at her for a few moments, drinking in her presence. He had no doubt his rakish history was in the past, that he had simply been waiting.

Waiting for her.

With a groan of surrender, he kissed her deeply, easing back to suck down a breath and smile at her. "If this is what happens every time you're in a library, I may have to make time for more reading."

"Less talk, more kisses," she commanded.

"More kisses," he muttered before doing exactly as she bid. That he could do. As he stripped off her clothes and admired her in the lamplight, he grinned to himself. Life with his wild wallflower would never be dull, of that he was certain.

THE END

Find more books by Samantha Holt on her website
www.samanthaholtromance.com
Read on for a sample of Waiting for a Rogue Like You

Chapter One

Rain beat upon the window. The fire beside Drake hissed as droplets seeped down the chimney. Wind buffeted the inn, making its presence known, slipping through the cracks in the window behind him and sending a chill down his spine. He tightened his muscles and forced away the shudder that threatened to wrack him. He hated nights like this.

He drained his ale and gestured to Louisa to bring him another. The tang of drink had long worn off and the gentle warmth of the alcohol had dissipated. He'd need something stronger before long if he was ever to sleep through the weather that was battering the coast of Cornwall. But his bed was a few hours away, so he'd save a healthy helping of whiskey until then.

"Bit late even for you, Drake," Louisa commented, whipping a cloth from her belt and wiping down the table before placing a mug of ale in front of him.

He grinned at the pretty barmaid. "Do you not enjoy my fine company?"

She gave him a knowing look. Louisa had always been somewhat immune to his charms. But then the owner of the Ship Inn knew him better than most in their small fishing village. With Louisa's help, he and the rest of his crew had skirted many a customs man.

"So long as you have coin, I enjoy your company just fine."

He shook his head. "And here I thought it was my fine looks and witty humor you liked me for."

"Some women might be charmed by your scarred face, Drake, but I prefer a man with a clean jaw and a sensible look about him."

He smirked. "Ale and insults. I wonder why I continue to come back here."

"Because"—she paused and tucked the cloth back into her belt— "I'm the only innkeeper who will have you."

A shout at the bar drew her attention from Drake, leaving him alone with his fresh ale. He lifted a finger and trailed it down the scar on his lip. A cold knot bunched in his stomach. He shook his head and dropped his hand away.

One scar hardly meant much. Besides, Louisa was right. Despite his limp and the scar, women found him more handsome than ever. The nice little air of danger seemed to draw them in with ease. At least he wasn't grizzled like Knight. That man was more scarred and ugly than any of their smuggling crew.

Drake took a quick swig of ale, closing his eyes briefly to feel it slide down his throat and settle in his gut, washing away the tightness there. He opened his eyes and met the gaze of a fair-haired wench, currently propped against a wall with a redheaded friend, looking bored indeed.

He crooked a finger at the woman and motioned to her friend. A little female company would pass the time until either the weather settled, and he could return to the ship or he passed out from drinking. Either would be acceptable but he'd rather fall asleep in a tangle of female limbs.

A smile curved the woman's lips and she pressed a hand to her friend's arm, drawing her attention to Drake. Both women sidled over, one draping herself immediately across his lap. She smelled of log fires and too much cheap perfume, but her body was soft against his and her breasts bountiful. The redhead woman drew a chair close and sat beside him, running a hand down one arm.

"You a soldier?" she asked.

"Not anymore."

The woman on his lap laughed. "Drake is a captain," she told her friend. "She's new here," she explained.

Drake dug through his memory for a name for the woman currently running her fingers through his hair. He knew most of the wenches who frequented the inn and the chances were he'd bedded her before but her name escaped him.

He flashed a grin at the friend. "Lucky for me."

"You want two tonight then?" The woman on his lap trailed her fingers down his chest, slipping into the open neckline of his shirt.

Her cool, slightly rough fingers made him shudder. Behind him, the rain beat against the glass. He nodded swiftly. "Two. Definitely." Hell, he'd have four or five if he could. On a night like this, being wrapped in a bundle of warm, female bodies was sounding more appealing by the second. "What's your name?" he asked the redhead.

"Anything you want it to be." She leaned in and stroked a hand down his chest. "He's strong."

The light-haired woman nodded. "Drake here is practically a gentleman, aren't you, Drake?"

"Rich, strong, and practically a gentleman," the woman cooed. "You should have a wife to go home to."

He chuckled and stroked a finger over the revealed shoulder of the redhead. "Why would I want a wife when I can enjoy the company of women like you?"

And many other women. Since returning from the war, he'd found it remarkably easy to sway women into bed. Not that he'd ever had any real difficulties but captaining a ship and a little gray around the temples had certainly helped. He grinned to himself. Gave him that worldly, dangerous look that combined so perfectly with the scar.

A gust of frigid air blew into the inn, riffling the fabric of the woman's gown. Leaves tumbled across the wooden floorboards and one came to a stop near Drake's boot. He glanced up at the newcomer.

Female. He straightened a little. A female in a fine gown. He peered around and noted he wasn't the only one to stir at the entrance of this stranger. Several other men followed her with their gazes as she passed by their tables.

He watched, breath held, waiting for an opportunity to glimpse her features. Tucked under a cloak, she carried herself like a woman who had been to a finishing school, head lifted, shoulders back, with a graceful elegance seldom seen in Cornish fishing villages. The women here had no time for worrying about their posture or how they walked.

She glanced around, and Drake straightened further. He'd known somehow. Know how beautiful she'd be. She pushed down the hood of the cloak, revealing black, glossy hair coiled carefully. A few loose, damp strands clung to her face and she pushed one away with a finger. Generous lips combined with large eyes and a profile that was as close to perfection as he'd ever seen. A bolt of need speared him, sending liquid heat through his body.

What the devil was a woman like that doing in an inn so late at night unchaperoned?

The woman stopped at the bar and leaned over to speak to Louisa. He could not hear the words exchanged, but Louisa shook her head and the lady made a frustrated noise. She slumped onto a stool at the bar and dropped her head to the wood, leaving her arms hanging limply at her side. She straightened herself quickly and seemed to shake herself out of whatever distress she had found herself in. He heard her ask Louisa for a sherry.

Well, if he ever saw a woman in distress, here was one. And Lord forbid he ignore a beautiful woman in need. He peeled away the female hands from his chest and fished out a few coins and handed them to the wenches. The fair-haired woman rolled her eyes.

"Can't keep Drake's attention for long," she explained to her friend. "Not when there's another pretty face around." She jerked her head toward the woman.

The redhead pouted. "A pity. Perhaps we can warm your bed another time, Drake."

He nodded. "How could I pass up on such an offer?" He winked at the redhead and waited for the woman on his lap to move before rising and snatching his ale.

He'd once loathed the thing but once he'd discovered it softened women toward him, he used it to good effect. He didn't need this woman's pity today, though, so he opted to keep his limp at a minimum.

Louise motioned to him when he approached the bar. "Drake, perhaps you might know where Knight is."

He lifted a brow and looked between the woman and Louisa. Up close, the stranger was pure perfection. Creamy skin, slightly dewy from the rain, flushed cheeks, a few delicate freckles across her nose, and lips that made him want to sink to his knees and beg to feel them on his skin. She mimicked his expression, lifting one dark eyebrow.

"What would a lady like you be wanting with Knight?"

"That is none of your business."

He'd been right. This was an educated woman. Potentially wealthy too. The finery of her clothing was even more apparent now he was a mere few steps away, and her accent was refined.

He shrugged and settled himself on the stood next to her. Louisa shot him a warning look that said 'play nicely' as she went to attend to two men by the fireplace. He flashed her a grin. He *always* played nicely. So nicely in fact, most women came back wanting more.

Drake gulped down some ale, watching her from the periphery of his vision. She kept her gaze pointedly ahead. "If you do not tell me what you want with Knight, I am not sure I can help."

Her head snapped around. Fire flared in her eyes. "I have had a long, tiring day. If you know something, I suggest you tell me immediately."

His lips quirked. "Is that a threat?"

"Yes." She sighed. "No." Her shoulders sagged. "I just need to know where Lewis is."

The hint of vulnerability in her posture pulled at some seldom tugged string inside him. He'd done heroics. Still did occasionally, though they rarely involved women. The smuggling ring for which he captained a ship was mostly a cover for their wartime involvement. Under the guise of nothing but lawless smugglers, he and three other men organized shipping goods and spies to help the war effort. However, that was about as heroic as he got since getting struck by shrapnel in battle. The pretty penny he earned smuggling goods in was the real benefit.

As much as he wanted to continue to toy with her, he could not. "Away on business, I'm afraid."

"You are an acquaintance of his?"

He nodded. "A friend I suppose. Though Knight might say otherwise."

The brooding hulk of a man had been brought on as the face of their smuggling efforts. He had a criminal look to him and hardly anyone knew a thing about him. Red, the Earl of Redmere, who had been the one to bring them together, knew little more than the rest of them, save that Lewis Knight's terrifying exterior saved them from many a scrape.

"When will he return? Where are his lodgings?"

"That is a more difficult question to answer, I'm afraid."

"If you are his friend, how do you not know where he is?"

Drake lifted a shoulder. "That's Knight for you. He likes to keep himself to himself."

She sighed again and tightened the cloak around her neck. When she made to leave, he put a hand to her arm. Her gaze shot up to his, her eyes reminding of him of luxurious, warm whiskey.

"It's a dark night."

Her lips curved. "Most nights are."

He chuckled. "It's cold and wet too. Why do you not join me for a drink by the fire? Dry off before venturing out again?"

"I did not come here for a drink." She slid off the stool and flipped up the hood of her cloak. "Particularly not with a man who enjoys the company of...well..." She slid a pointed look toward the women who had found another couple of men to occupy them.

"I see I am to have my previous sins held against me." He stood and straightened. "But regardless, you should not be out there alone. Many unsavory sorts frequent nights like these. It's not safe for a woman like yourself."

"I have travelled a long way alone, sir, and dealt with many unsavory sorts." Her lips tilted. "Some even worse than you."

He shook his head with a grin. Her bold stance combined with the dash of fire in her eyes had him off balance—not the sort of position in which a man with a damaged leg needed to be.

"You would put yourself in danger to spite me? A man you do not know?"

The woman ran her gaze over him. "I see more danger to my person here."

He could not deny that. Every part of him ran hot with need. The spark had ignited into an inferno as soon as she'd opened her mouth and looked at him with such disdain. If she remained in his company, he could not guarantee he'd remain a gentleman.

Not that she thought him one in the first place.

"Now, if you will excuse me..." She nodded toward the women. "I shall leave you to your female company. No doubt they would prefer your companionship to their current friends."

"Then you admit there is something a woman might like about my company?"

"Not *this* woman."

She gave him no chance to respond, striding toward the door, pulling it open and stepping out into the night. He opened his mouth then shut it, sinking back onto the stool.

Well, blast. His charms had utterly failed him. However, if she was looking for Knight he might well see her again. Perhaps next time, he would be able to make a better impression. What an attractive, refined woman like her would want with a beast of a man like Knight, however, he did not know.

A knife of dread jabbed into his gut when two of the patrons stood. They conferred for a moment then nodded to each other before leaving the inn. Men like that did not leave in the middle of a storm—not without purpose.

And he had a strong suspicion what that purpose was.

The woman.

He sighed and snatched up his jacket from his original seat. It looked like he'd be seeing the woman sooner than he thought.

Made in the USA
Columbia, SC
31 October 2019